Teething Trouble

Teething Trouble

Philip Edwards

Published by Tablo

Published in 2020 by Tablo Publishing.

Publisher and wholesale enquiries: orders@tablo.io

20 21 22 23 LSC 10 9 8 7 6 5 4 3 2 1

DEDICATION

For Richard, Elinor, Ian, Stephanie and Ceri and for all of their children and grandchildren.....Oh, and for Mr. Hawkins, the best dentist in the world.

Thanks
Dyfed Davies, my old boss. Thanks for sub-editing this story and the thousands of end-of-year reports that passed through our hands.

Also to Sue Rundle-Hughes for the wonderful front cover art.

THE BEGINNING.

A novel aimed at 9-11 years old children.

"Don't you mess around with tooth fairies, oh no, not with them," she whispered harshly. "You give them the respect that they rightly deserve. They take something from you that you don't need and they give something in return but don't you mess with them. They can be nasty and they can hold a grudge. Nearly the death of me they were. You listen to me well. Don't mess with tooth fairies. Pillow your tooth and spend the money on something for yourself and nobody else. If I were you, I'd be careful what you say when you're near a gnome. I really wouldn't trust further than I can spit."

PROLOGUE

There was a large tear in Granny Beth's eye on the day that I told her that I knew the truth about Santa Clause. She took one of her dainty lace handkerchiefs to wipe it away, then she took my hand and guided me to her garden. We looked out towards the park, a sparkling lake and down the valley towards the family factory. A pair of mallard ducks swooped overhead, turning gently in the distance, making for an elegant splashdown in the calm waters. She turned towards me, looking deeply into my eyes and explained, "Has your mum ever said to you that if you don't behave yourself, if you are naughty then Santa won't be coming to visit you?" I nodded gently, starting to get worried. Wiping away the last trace of tear, she added, "Well, that's true," and she nodded wisely. " Parents of naughty, nasty children get sent a letter from The North Pole. Oh yes, they do you know. I've seen them. It comes on a deep black paper, black as night it is, and the writing is in a glowing green ink. It tells the parents that all Santa deliveries have been cancelled because of the behaviour of that child." Squeezing my hand quite hard, she continued, "It even lists all of the naughty things that the child has done. Believe me, sometimes the list is enormous. Sometimes there is only one naughty item on the list, but that can be enough, believe me." Pausing a while to fold her handkerchief she continued, " When that happens, most parents are deeply saddened but they know that there is no turning back on the decision. So, from that moment on, they pretend that they are Santa. Some even dress the part. They creep into the child's bedroom, quiet as mice, to deliver the toys on Christmas morning."

"Oh stop telling fibs Granny Beth, " I squealed. "You don't expect me to believe that do you? You'll be expecting me to believe in ghosts, pixies and the Loch Ness Monster next."

"Oh come come," she nodded, tapping my knee. "You really must try to be more open minded," and with that, she gave me a smile and whispered to me, " I was never naughty. Maybe misguided once but no, never was I naughty and because of that, Santa still delivers to me right to this day." At this, I noticed a delightful sparkle in her now dry eyes.

"Seriously?" I asked. "Do you seriously expect me to believe that? You'll be expecting me to believe in gnomes and tooth fairies next."

Suddenly, she took a sharp inward gasp. Her manner changed completely and she stared straight into my eyes. She had turned deathly pale and was starting to shake. "Don't you mess around with tooth fairies, oh no, not with them," she whispered harshly. "You give them the respect that they rightly deserve. They take something from you that you don't need and they give something in return but don't you mess with them. They can be nasty and they can hold a grudge. Nearly the death of me they were, if it hadn't been for my mum. You listen to me well. Don't mess with tooth fairies. Pillow your tooth and spend the money on something for yourself and nobody else. If I were you, I'd be careful what you say when you're near a gnome. I really wouldn't trust further than I can spit."

Grasping my hand firmly, she took me to a garden bench and sat me down. "Let me tell you a story. My story and your grandfather Barnaby's story. A story from our childhood, when a silver ten pence coin would buy a large bar of chocolate and when fifty pence would keep you in chocolate until you were sick of it."

She did too. She told me a story that took us back to her childhood, to Grandad Barnaby's childhood, to the story of two horrible family accidents, gloves, and of a strange little man that kept rats. By the end, with the sun setting over the lake, I was totally spellbound.....and I hope you will be too.

Robin Spruddge.
2016

CHAPTER 1.

The Darkest of Days.

The day started like the weather, dreary and dark. The long Christmas break was over. Time to get back to school and a new term. The heart and soul of many a schoolboy and girl lay dark with despair this morning. The glittery gloss had long been worn off the festive cheer. Aunts, uncles and grandparents, with their kipper ties, super hero socks and Parisienne bath salts had all returned home to store their unwanted gifts for re-distribution next year. New toys had lost their initial sparkle, batteries had flattened and for Beth Saunders, the only hope for the future was the possibilities offered by Granny Devereaux's Book Token gift.

She lay there, all comfy and cosy under her blankets. She loved the smell of the lavender expelled from her pillowcase and she knew that her fresh clothes and her handkerchief would smell just the same - just as soon as she raised herself to get dressed.

She heard her mother calling from the kitchen.

“Beth, Beth dear. Orange or apple juice?"

"Apple please, Mummy.”

Beth pulled her bedding up under her chin. Just a few more luxurious moments of holiday time to indulge in before 'back to school' misery kicked in. Just a few more lingering moments to share with her Princess Pink wallpaper and matching curtains. Just one deliciously longer warm minute whilst trying to cast away the sound of the wind and the rain outside. And it was a Friday. Who on Earth believed that going back to school on a Friday was a good idea? Just one day at school, then another weekend off! Just crazy! Whose idea was that anyway?

"Beth!!!!! Beth!!! Get up you lazy lump! Breakfast is on the table. Boiled egg, toast for soldiers, fruit juice and some cornflakes.

Slowly, deliberately, enjoying the very last seconds of the freedom that Christmas had given her, she reluctantly folded her legs over the side of the bed. Then all at once, she became far more awake and alert. There was something not quite right in her mouth! It just didn't feel quite right or the same as normal. Her tongue wheedled around a bit and found the toothy gap that had been created the night before. She'd been sitting near her Christmas tree, reading by fairy-light whilst chewing on a piece of toffee when suddenly she'd felt a sharp pain! She'd spat out the toffee and noticed blood and a small speck of white. A live tooth – that was now dead! That wiggly tooth that had been troubling her for weeks had finally lost its battle with Beth's gums. Without thinking, Beth reached under her pillow and there it was - a sparkling silver coin and a receipt. It read:-

CERTIFICATE

TEETHING TROUBLE TOOTH FAIRIES INC.

This Certifies that

Beth Saunders

Has successfully pillowed one Class A tooth

FIFTY PENCE

January 4th 1963
DATE

Ivory Cuspid
OPERATIVE

She gazed outside thinking. Were there really tooth fairies, or was it just her mummy playing grown-up tricks? No matter how long she stared though, the bright, shiny coin and the receipt remained there besides the pillow. Fifty pence and a tiny signed receipt. Between Granny

Devereaux's book token and Ivory Cuspid's tooth money, she would indeed be looking forward to her visit to the book shop next weekend.

Downstairs at the breakfast table, Beth's mum broke the top off her egg as Beth discreetly placed a few breadcrumbs in her pocket.

"Beth, I'll know when you'll be grown up. It'll be the day that you break the top off of your own egg!" Her mum smiled, giving her daughter a wink.

Beth answered with a toothy grin. "Thanks Mum, and thanks for thuch a thplendid breakfatht."

"I beg your pardon?" gasped her mum; her face breaking into a smile.

"Oh No!" bellowed Beth. "That tooth. Sinth I lotht the tooth I've developed a lithp. What will the other children thay. I can't go to school like thith . They just won't take me theriouthly any more."

Beth's mum found it very hard indeed not to giggle at this little outburst but she knew that would totally destroy her daughter's confidence at this moment in time. Still, it continued to be hard not to smile.

"Thtop thmirking mother. It's thimply not funny!" Beth replied.

"Whisper. Talk in a whisper.....then nobody will notice. Besides, I can already see you're new tooth coming through. You'll be right as rain in just a few weeks." reassured her mum!

"WEEKTH!!!" exclaimed Beth.

"Hurry up now, finish your breakfast. Here's your packed lunch. Oh! and by the way. A quiet word Beth. A few weeks ago Mrs. Tomlinson at the shop said she'd seen you walking to school with that Spruddge boy from the brown side. Do you think it's a good idea to hang about with him?"

"Muu uum. I sometimes meet him on the way to thchool. Thometimes we talk. He'th a nice lad you know despite his mother. He'th sort of sweet. You know, we have thomething in common" Beth explained.

Beth's gaze drifted to the silver trophy on the top of her piano. It was her dad's last golf trophy for scoring a hole-in-one. She kept it in sparkling condition by polishing it every Saturday in the forlorn hope that some small memory of her dad would come back to her. Beth had been just a little less than two years old on the fateful day that the 'act of God' had happened. Try as she may, there were no memories of him in her head. Her dad, Arthur Saunders, had been a very keen golfer. On the tragically fateful day he'd been participating in a championship team event at his beloved golf club. Arthur was in fantastic form that day. Everything was going so well for him. On the eighteenth hole, he faced a challenging par 3 hole and had teed off using his trusty four iron. Whack! Arthur had driven the ball straight and true, watching it arc towards the distant hole. However, simultaneously, without any warning, as his four iron reached the top of his follow through and pointed towards the overcast sky there was one almighty flash, followed by

"Fffffffeeeeerwhop. BBBOOOOOMMM!"

The biggest, loudest thunder-clap ever heard on the course rang out - except Arthur sadly never heard it. A spectacular lightning bolt had reached out from the grey sky and struck his four iron sending 1,000,000,000,000 watts surging through his body and earthing out through his brand new Stubert Comfort Pro Waterproof Golf Shoes - practically welding them to the ground. Arthur tragically was no more. His shocked fellow golfers are reported to have said: "He never felt a thing before he hit the floor."

Arthur hadn't survived to celebrate the outcome of his last shot. It had turned out to be a tournament and trophy winning shot of pure genius – a hole-in-one no less. Over passing years, the shot had assumed legendary status amongst the golfing members of the club. "Arthur's Tee Shot of Doom" they called it and a small plaque had been placed at the very tee where he'd met his end.

"Yes, I know, Beth." replied Mrs. Saunders, bringing Beth back from her day-dream. "It must be comforting for you to talk to somebody else who has lost their dad in tragic circumstances......but Beth...we've certain standards to maintain in the top part of town you know."

Beth lived in what was locally called 'high town', near the park. Most of her adult neighbours worked in the offices of the local glove factory – a thriving company. Many spent their days processing orders and working on accounts – often performing mathematical miracles. They could calculate a sum and by the time the bill had found its way to the end of the accounting room a zero would find its way onto the end of the starting number. It's truly amazing how much money could be made by just moving paper.

Beth grabbed her coat and her school bag, hugged her mum and wished her a good day, then walked out into the unwelcoming dreariness of the January morn. Stepping through the garden gate she turned onto the path through the park. Beth's school walk took a delightful tour of the posh part of her little town. Walking past the slide and the swings, her route took a quarter turn around a sparkling lake. She lingered there for a moment and in no time, her favourite pair of mallards spotted her and shot across the lake as fast as their little webbed feet would take them.

"There you go," whispered Beth and she fed them the crumbs saved from the breakfast table - they dabbled through the water enjoying their routine treat.

The lake measured about a quarter of a mile around its perimeter. During the Spring, a proud row of apple and cherry blossom trees lined the banks. Pink and white blossom would make a stunning reflection in the water making the lake a popular spot with young courting couples. Later, the blossom would fall like snow forming small white drifts. January however brought its own delights. Often ice would form and the lake would freeze over. When that happened, you could skim a stone across the surface and a peculiar, haunting shrieking noise would echo across the lake and through the park. Remembering the gap in her teeth, Beth felt certain that if there actually were such things as tooth fairies, then this is the place where they would build their castles.

Turning onto a path to her right, she next passed the tennis courts and the bowling green. That concluded the best part of her journey. Town came next, past Lesley's department store, the cinema and the church. She had a quick look at the bookshop display but at the moment it mostly featured books on fishing. Hopefully, she'd find something more suitable on her Saturday spending spree. Finally Beth started wandering down a steep avenue towards the school gates. She checked her shiny new Christmas watch. Half past eight. Using her fingers in her pocket to help her count, she reluctantly realised that meant seven hours to endure until freedom returned. Seven and a half hours in the company of her teacher, Mr. Fortitude Jones. She could hardly contain herself.

CHAPTER 2.

Spruddge, spruddgers and spruddges.

Barnaby Spruddge lay on his straw filled mattress enjoying that pleasant feeling of doziness that arrives at the end of a night's sleep. Pulling a blanket of sacking up towards his neck, he tried to drive out the smell of the river and the glove factory, a vile odour that crept into every inch of his bare bedroom. "Cleaning out the tanning vats I suppose," he daydreamed. "That's going to spoil my walk to school. Hope Ma has brought the washing in. The Brown Town walk to school, on a gloomy Friday morning in Winter". Pulling the blanket tightly around him and squeezing himself into a hollow in his mattress, he tried to put the image of his journey past the smelly river and the stinking glove factory out of his head.

"GETTOUTCHAABEDRIGHTNOW! You naughty, nasty, ne'er-do-well." bellowed Ma Spruddge as she dragged the rough, old woollen blanket from her half-starved child.

Barnaby, instantly awake shot out of his straw-filled mattress. He knew from experience that he had no more than five seconds to avoid a beating, a drenching from a saucepan of ice-cold water, or even both. He could never quite decide which was worse. A beating hurt like the blazes, especially when Ma Spruddge was in a mood. A drenching didn't hurt but then you had a wet mattress for days afterwards. He leapt from his bed and was up and dressed before his blanket had even settled on the floor. Barnaby could move fast when he needed to. Sometimes it was like watching a terrier. He could be somewhere, then between a clock's tick, he'd be somewhere else. This drove old Ma Spruddge wild but stealth was Barnaby's best defence against the fearsome leather belt.

"Hey, you dozy daydreamer," shouted Ma. "You going to eat your breakfast? You don't think I'm slaving over a hot stove just for you to stare into space do you?"

Porridge again. Porridge mixed with hot water and a little salt. Strangely, it tasted just like porridge mixed with hot water and a little salt. Vile. Oh how Barnaby longed for a decent breakfast. Some hot buttered toast with marmalade, bacon, egg and sausage. Fresh orange juice - now that would be a real treat. A breakfast just like the ones that he sometimes saw the heroes in his comics having, but sadly not for him. Salty porridge had been his breakfast ever since Dad had gone. At least when Dad was alive he'd get a boiled egg on Sunday mornings.

"And I bet you haven't cleaned your father's spruddge, you lazy lump." smirked old Ma Spruddge. "Only thing we've got left of your dad. Least we can do is keep it clean in his honour."

"Not the only thing that we have left," muttered Barnaby under his breath, "still got his belt haven't you."

"WHATCHASAY,"

"I said that I'd cleaned the spruddge last Sunday, just like I clean it every Sunday ma."

"I hope you cleaned the little brass label, the one that says 'Hope Gloves for Gentrified Ladies', with Brasso. "

"With Brasso," answered Barnaby, joining in the chorus.

"Bet you forgot to polish the little silver badge, the one that says, 'Stanley Spruddge, Leading Spruddge Operative. Proud of that badge was your dad. L.S.O. at the glove factory was your dad, just like you grandfather and your great-grandfather."

"and the grandfathers before that," added Barnaby.

"Yes, like them all. Gave us a bit more status than most of the folk here in Brown Town. Yes, they all might be working in the glove factory. Squeegers, rinsers, washers but they all held their head up to an L.S.O. Oh yes they did you know. A cut above he was. Knew his spruddge well and bright enough to be left in charge of the spruddger gang when the chief spruddger operative was absent."

Barnaby looked over at the gleaming spruddge, propped up against the doorway. It looked a bit like a garden fork, but with three wooden prongs, looking much like an old-fashioned milking stool with a handle.

"I bet you forgot to put the oils and polish back were they belong. You're always forgetting that."

"No ma. I put them in the box in the shed by the vegetable patch. Just like I do every Sunday." replied Barnaby in much the same way as he did when they had this weekly conversation. "It's not looking good down there Ma. Thistles and bindweed everywhere."

"What about them cabbages that I planted? Those ones by the rhubarb."

"Dead." answered Barnaby. "Slugs had them."

"What about the turnips. I bet them turnips are growing. Nothing can kill a turnip."

"No, they're dead too. Greenfly I think." replied Barnaby.

"Loved that vegetable patch did your dad. His pride and joy they were. Loved his cabbages and onions. His marrows, huge they were. They'd win prizes in the local show they would. Oh how the other gardeners would look up to him. Every summer, his beans would almost block out the sun. Thanks to his vegetables, every summer and autumn, we'd eat like royalty we would."

Turning her head towards the door, she gazed at the spruddge again.

"He knew that spruddge like his own right arm you know. Every night he'd carry it home on his shoulder he would. Hard to believe that considering where it had been but he always cleaned it before coming home. Day after day, he shoved it into the tanning vat, churning, turning the mix like an Indian chef mixing a saucepan of Chicken Bhoona. He'd hold on to the handle of the spruddge as the three prongs turned the leather, round and round, swirling and churning, never letting the mix keep still. Watched him working a few times. They let me tip my bucket into the vat they did. He looked like a conductor working his orchestra he did. I was so proud of him I was."

Barnaby passed her a rag to wipe the tears from her eyes. He'd been here before. He knew what was expected of him.

"Just last year it was," sniffled old Ma Spruddge. "July the eighteenth when the knock came to my door. They had huuuuuge tears in their eyes they did. They did say that it was quick though. Oh, it was hot that day. The fumes from the vat had spread all over Brown Town. Stinking to high heaven it was. Nobody could put their washing out that day, oh no." she continued as Barnaby lovingly placed his hand on her arm to comfort her. "They said a large bubble of gas had formed deep in the heart of one of the vats. As it rose to the surface, a clump of leather wrapped itself around your poor dad's spruddge. Silly old Stanley though, he didn't want to let go of his spruddge did he. That spruddge that had been passed down from his father, his father's father and all of the fathers before them," snuffled Old Ma Spruddge, with Barnaby joining in the chorus again. "It had sentimental value didn't it. I bet he was thinking about the cost of a replacement spruddge. After all, a quality spruddge cost good money. The sort of money that we can ill afford. AND besides, he couldn't have faced explaining his lost spruddge to old Ma Spruddge, no indeed! Stanley stubbornly refused to let go of his prized possession –Oh no. It was part of his family's long and proud history. So, sadly just like some other unfortunate spruddgers before him, he got sucked into the vat and drowned – holding firm to the family spruddge. Wouldn't let go would he."

"Couldn't they save him ma?" asked Barnaby knowing that he'd heard the answer a dozen times before.

"Not so much couldn't save him as wouldn't save him. Four lads had seen it happen didn't they but there's an unwritten rule at the side of the tanning vat. 'If you go in the vat, then in the vat you stay.' If anybody had jumped in after him, then they would have drowned too. Besides, if you go into that mix the smell would never leave you. Nobody would ever want to be near you again. Believe me, loneliness can easily be a fate worse than death."

"SSSSSSSNNNNNNNNNNNNNNNIIFFFFFFFFFF..........THHHHHHRRRRP." as she blew her nose, making the sort of sound that would have been the pride and joy of the trombone section of any brass band.

"Then the knock came on my door. Three days later it was."

"Three days," agreed Barnaby, just as he did whenever they had this conversation.

"Three days later, those lads came carrying your dad's spruddge. Oh, they'd tried to clean it I know but nobody could clean that spruddge the way that you dad could. Took us days to get it proper clean."

"Days." agreed Barnaby, wiping a tear from his mum's eye with the snot sodden rag.

"So there it stands besides the door now, waiting the time when you take that spruddge and follow your father's footsteps, and your grandfathers' and all the great-grandfather's before that."

"Great-grandfather's before that," nodded Barnaby as the hopelessness of their situation became clear. Now, every single day old Ma Spruddge walked the streets of Hope carrying her bucket and shovel, collecting *The* Pure:- the dog poo which formed the key ingredient inside the leather tanning vat. Barnaby just waited until he was old enough to shoulder the spruddge. There he sat at the bare kitchen table as his mother sobbed and sobbed, doing his best to comfort her, helping her to blow her nose and wiping away her tears, the sort of tears that could fill an ocean.

They were both pulled back from their gloom by the sound of the spruddgers marching down the street, singing their spruddging song, on their way to their daily toil at the glove factory.

See the merry Spruddgers swirl,
give the mix, a tremendous twirl.
Squishing and scrunching and squeezing it through,
a really revolting repulsive brew.

See the merry Spruddgers swirl,
making the gloves for many a girl
or lady to wear at the finest ball
for her to beguile and entrance them all.

See the merry Spruddgers swirl,
As they watch their factory flag unfurl.
Remember our friends that fell in the mix
drowning's the fate the vat inflicts.

Barnaby had heard that song so many times. It echoed along the brown side of the river most days as he wandered home from school.

"Doesn't sound so good without your dad, does it." snuffled Ma. "Missing his high tenor voice they are. Lovely voice he had did your dad. That song sounded happy when your dad was around even though they were marching to such a dreadful job.It brought a little joy into their troubled world. Sad now. Sad and and slow – more like a funeral."

It certainly made Barnaby sad thinking that every day he heard it was one day closer to the time he'd actually join them and take his dad's place.

"Ma. Remember the money that I had from the tooth fairy last Friday?" Barnaby queried tentatively.

"Lords above. You've never still got that ten pence. I'd have thought that a scoundrel like you would have had a hole burned in his pocket by now. What you keeping that for anyway? That young lass up the posh end? You can forget that right away. That Beth girl; far too posh for the likes of you." Ma remarked with a sneer.

Barnaby sighed. "I was thinking of buying some eggs for both of us actually. We could have a nice eggy soldier breakfast ..... like when Dad was around."

"Aaaaaaaargh!" screamed Ma as her face turned a shade of death. "YOU want to spend YOUR tooth fairy money on ME? After what happened to ME last time. You know that's against the tooth fairy rule. Look at what happened to ME last time," giving Barnaby a horrible toothless grin. "There I was, starving half to death after your father....that dozy lump....left us....and there I was with nowhere to go, so I took your tooth fairy money...... just to buy some bread......and why couldn't he have taken more care with his spruddging anyway? .....Starving I was....we were....just for a loaf of bread.....and that very night, just as my head touched the pillow and I wakes up and not a single tooth in my head. Not a single one. It was the fairies it was. Mark my words, it was the fairies that did it. Oh yes, very nice and sweet they can be but they have a nasty side you now. A mean, nasty side. I'll never be able to play my clarinet now, not never. You remember the rule me lad? Remember the Fairy Rule? Remember it well, and she gazed skywards and chanted.

fairy silver 'neath the pillow fold,
is for the child alone to hold.
If silver goes to the daddy or mummy,
'til the day they die, they'll be awfully gummy.

Barnaby didn't quite know what to believe when it came to the tooth fairy. Lots of his classmates were convinced that they didn't exist and that their parents sneaked the money under their pillows whilst they were actually sleeping. It all sounded very possible but it left Barnaby with a couple of questions like why on earth would Ma Spruddge leave money under Barnaby's pillow when her purse held nothing but emptiness. Also, if it had come from her purse then why was she so certain that she wouldn't take a share.

It was all so mysterious and odd. You know, you even got a receipt for a tooth. Barnaby felt in his pocket and there was his receipt together with his shining fairy money. The receipt read:-

Teething Troubles Tooth Fairies
Inc
One Class D Tooth
10p
Operative
Keith the Teeth

"Finished? Then stop day dreaming and get yourself off to school and don't forget, if you see any of *The Pure* along the way, you make sure you bring it back." instructed Ma.

Barnaby nodded as he forced down his last spoonful of salty porridge. He grabbed his coat and struggled to get it on. He'd noticeably grown upwards last summer but thankfully not outwards. As a direct result, his arms were now longer than the distance between the coat's arm-pits and the pockets. He could no longer put his hands in his pockets unless he bent his arms a little. His scarf; Barnaby loved it, as it used to belong to his dad was a deep green and blue of very old fashioned stripes. Just like his dad's spruddge this had also been passed down through the family. Thankfully, Stanley Spruddge hadn't been wearing the scarf on that fateful day. Although it had not one ounce of fashion or style attached to it, it kept Barnaby warm in the winter and anything that could do that was a real blessing.

Outside was dark and dreary. A light but persistent cold drizzle fell from the direction of the Hope Glove factory. Thankfully a light breeze was blowing towards the factory now making the air feel clearer and relatively odour less. He walked northwards, catching an occasional glimpse of the river as it made its way past the factory on its slow journey to the sea. He passed The Morgue; a dark, sinister place. He'd once asked Ma what they did in there.

"Where they store the dead bodies, ...the ones that they manage to get out of the tanning vats, ...not like that dozy dad of yours. Those that die in suspicious circumstances too. They get put in there too whilst things get investigated." Ma said more in a secret whisper than out loud. She then drew closer to Barnaby and again whispered in a hushed, secretive tones. "Last week, Edgar Spokeshave from up the road did his work experience there. His mum said that it had been very quiet for him. Sometimes.......too quiet. He'd wished it had been a bit more exciting. He'd have loved to have worked the night shift, but they wouldn't let him".

Next along his route there was The Rat Farm where an eccentric elderly gent actually bred rats. He arranged for them to be delivered to the local medical research centre to be experimented upon. This journey was strictly a one-way trip for the rats. Barnaby hated rats and he hated this particular part of his journey. The rats were always agitated as though they sensed the fate that awaited them. Always squeaking, always rustling about, never still. Barnaby never quite understood why the rat man ever bothered to farm rats, after all there were plenty running around the lower part of town.

The building itself was just an old tin shanty that looked dark and dirty. Cobwebs and grime covered the window frames. The mark of a stray football could clearly be seen on one pane, from a long, forgotten child dribbling his way to school. Suddenly, a ragged net curtain was forcibly pulled to one side. There was the rat man, Mr. Simpkins. A dinky, thin man with curiously pointed features and protruding teeth. Teeth. Yes, but only three of them. He still had two teeth sticking outwards from his top gum, matched by one crooked, stained tooth on the bottom gum. You know how it is that people say that a dog's owner often looks like their dog. Well, if you took one look at The Rat Man, you would have no doubt about his choice of pets. He started waving wildly at Barnaby through the window and then started knocking on the filthy glass.

"Oh no," thought Barnaby, alarmed by the frightening sight, his shoulders sinking so low that his school bag slid slowly downwards to the muddy floor. He felt his heart sinking too, actually feeling it moving downwards, weighed down with with the miserable thought of what he knew what was coming next. The door to the rat farm burst open and there stood The Rat Man, dressed all in grey:- grey trousers held up by a bit of rope and a tatty grey pullover tucked in firmly at the middle. The legs of his trousers were also bound up with rope, "Just in case of an escaped rat I suppose." thought Barnaby.

"Just the man I wanted," wheezed Mr. Simpkins. "Indeed, the very man indeed. Tell me young Spruddge. How are you keeping these days? Busy? Just wondering, you free Saturday morning? About 11? You wouldn't be free would you? Or would you?"

"What's the problem Mr. Simpkins?" responded Barnaby nervously.

"Well, not a problem at all. No, not a problem. Maybe an opportunity though, an opportunity for you young fellow-me-lad. Yes, an opportunity."

"You want me to take some rats down to the science laboratory don't you?" Barnaby replied with a resigned sigh.

"Blow me down, yes blow me down. Blow me down I say. This boy can see into the future. The future I say." He sidled up to Barnaby and whispered into his ear, "See into the future hey....don't suppose you know anything about horse racing would you?"

"How many?" inquired Barnaby.

"Just one ......the winner of the Gold Cup would be really nice." Replied Mr Simpkins.

"No, not horses, how many rats?" exclaimed Barnaby.

"Just two. Two of my fine beauties. Two males. Waldo and Horace." informed Simpkins.

"You name them." gasped Barnaby. "You name them even though they are going to ......"

"Ssssshhhh," whispered Mr. Simpkins through his rat-like teeth. He clasped his filthy hands over Barnaby's mouth. "Ssssshhhh, Don't say the

D word. They'll know, you know," and he tipped a wink towards the cages at the rear.

Barnaby gently pushed the hand away. "Don't worry Mr. Simpkins. I'll be here at 11. I won't let you down."

"Fine. Excellent. I knew I could rely on you.....and remember, there'll be something in it for you. Always is. Well done young fellow-me-lad. See you Saturday." Said Mr Simpkins rubbing his dirty hands together.

Next along his walk to school came the clay pit. Just here, the path took a steep dip towards the valley floor.There was an easier way to get down this part of the hillside but the clay pit was a good shortcut , at the expense of just a little danger. It was a steep slope, covered with sticky, wet, orange clay. The significant challenge he faced was that, during winter time it tended to be very, very slippery. You had two options – you either had to focus on each and every footstep as if it would be your last, or you could use a more devil may care approach and sort of ski through the mud hoping that you were still upright and in one piece at the bottom. If you slipped or fell, and trust me you really didn't want to take a tumble on the clay pit, then you'd end up cut, bruised and covered with sort of an orange coloured stain. Barnaby knew that a slip on the clay pit would result in a yelling from Ma, followed by a good hard beating with the belt.

"HOWMANYTIMESHAVEIGOTCHATELLYOU? Don't (Slap!) go sliding down (Bop!) the clay (Pow!) pit (Zap!). Go (Smack!) the sensible(Thwack!) way! (Wham!)

Nigel Rivett's bungalow was just off the normal and sensible route to school. Routinely, Barnaby tried at all costs to avoid meeting Nigel whenever possible – as it often meant trouble if he did. It was acknowledged by everyone that Nigel Rivettt was not *the best fighter in the class* - although he definitely had the edge on Barnaby. However, he certainly wasn't as fast as Barnaby. In fact, in last year's Sports Day Barnaby had beaten Nigel in the 100m race by at least ten metres. Thankfully no major incident had spoiled the relationship between the two boys. You see, Nigel was a bit of a *wheeler dealer.* He'd buy things off other children and somehow always managed to sell them on at a profit. Comic Club was his top wheeze at the moment. All the lads from his class would meet in his garden to swop comics. Barnaby wanted and needed to be in Comic Club because he was hardly ever able to afford new comics. Comic Club meant that you'd manage to get to read new comics every few weeks without actually spending too much money. The hard reality of the club, however, was that Rivett took his cut of the action :- approximately 10%. When you walked into his garden then straight away, Rivett would take one of your comics as his cut……AND, he'd always take the best one…..the cleanest one, the shiniest one, the one that still smelled of comicy newness.

Of course, there was another reason why he wanted to avoid Rivett today. It involved Barnaby's recently sprained arm and a crepe bandage sling. Putting everything together, Barnaby decided to risk the Clay Pit, not knowing that it would prove to be quite a good decision. Well at least good in parts.

CHAPTER 3.

The Deal.

Thankfully Barnaby managed to reach the bottom of the slope unscathed. On this occasion there had been a particularly slippery part about half way down but he had managed to skid past that not only without falling but actually looking quite cool; as though he was an accomplished downhill ski champion. It was quite a shame really that there had been nobody around to stare in wonder and applaud his breakneck do or die style - but hey ho. On the other hand, if he had slipped in front of a large critical audience, no doubt there would have many very willing to judge his performance or lack of technique.

As he continued on his familiar journey, he was just walking past the glove factory entrance when his sharp eye suddenly spotted it. A rare treasure indeed, just lying there glistening with morning dew - speckled here and there with flecks of dust. He looked around to make sure nobody could see him. No, to his knowledge, there was nobody around. Thankfully, this particular morning there would be no unseen witnesses. He reached inside his pocket and pulled out a small, black plastic bag. Moving efficiently in a rehearsed manner he knew the routine he was about to follow well after several years of practice.

Down.

Scoop it.

Turn it.

Twist it.

Knot it.

Pocket it.

All efficiently done, in one well rehearsed routine Anyone watching his movements would have been reminded of a fine tuned machine or of a graceful Russian ballerina – as he swiftly scooped into action. It was indeed a well planned routine built upon the experience of rehearsal in trying to make an unpleasant task into something that would even have impressed gymnastic judges. Ma Spruddge would be so proud of unexpected find. A bag of white. Maybe he'd now get an egg on Sunday? Nobody, not even vets, actually knew why it happened but occasionally a dog would produce white poo. This was a pretty rare commodity and highly sought after and prized by the H.G.G.L. factory. Barnaby remembered his dad telling him in graphic detail that there was a special, small vat kept just for making white leather gloves. These particular gloves were highly prized and sought after by very rich ladies – due to the gloves being so exclusive and rare. His dad had called them *'the more money than sense ladies.'* As a direct result of his luck, Ma Spruddge would be able sell it and fetch a tidy sum for Barnaby's treasure. This lucky event left him with a broad smile. He just needed to remember to to avoid the coat pocket when his right hand grew cold.

Barnaby turned the last corner along his eventful journey. He could see the wrought iron school gate just slightly ajar ahead of him– enough of a gap for a single child to pass through safely. It appeared as if the gap had been created by someone on purpose as the gate was routinely wide open at this time of day. He also recognised Beth just heading towards the same school gate. She appeared to be checking her watch and doing some adding with her fingers. Barnaby gave her a welcoming smile and a knowing nod and she in turn smiled back. Suddenly, a thoroughly threatening figure stepped into view. A tall and quite alarming figure with hair combed into a mock Mohican hairstyle. Nigel Rivett. AND, he didn't look happy.

Rivett had clearly been responsible for the partly closed the gate. He had been hiding and waiting behind it but he now stepped right in front of Barnaby, completely filling the space between the gate and the gate post.

"Well hello Spruddgey, Happy New Year. Have you got it?"

At school everybody affectionately called Barnaby *Spruddgey*. It was a 'sweet' little pet name brought about when all of the other children had one day discovered that Barnaby was quite a tricky name to pronounce. The name stuck like glue. Complaining just added to the frequent use of the name. Strange that they didn't call him Porridge after all, he ate enough of it. Privately, Barnaby hated the name but at the same time he decided to grin and bear it; after all, they could have dreamed up something far worse.

"Have I got what?" asked Barnaby.

"The sling of course. The sling for my arm." Rivett squealed impatiently.

"No I haven't. My arm's better now so Ma took it away. Anyway, the deal was for six weeks. Six weeks have passed now, haven't they?" explained Barnaby in a matter of fact manner.

"Yes, that's right. Six weeks " replied Rivett abruptly, then added as if in self explanation, "But the last two weeks were Christmas holiday weeks. You can't count them. We made a deal. I should now get another two weeks use of the sling."

Beth, having just entered the school grounds immediately before Barnaby, had heard the conversation and being a somewhat nosey sort of character couldn't help but ask, "What kind of deal have you made? If you've made a deal with HIM, you know it will bring nothing but trouble."

Barnaby whispered, "Do you remember that for the last few weeks at school Rivett had his arm in a sling?"

Beth gently nodded recollecting the event clearly. She was aware of the fact that there were certain words that were *'lisp safe'*. 'Yes,' wasn't one of them.

"Well that wasn't his sling. It was my sling. Remember I slipped on the Clay Pit on the way home. I sprained my arm. Ma put it in a sling so it wouldn't hurt so much. When I wore it to school, Rivett saw it and offered me a deal."

"A deal? What sort of deal?" puzzled Beth.

"He wanted to use my sling so he could get out of doing any writing of course. Fooled Sir completely - didn't he. He had four weeks off, playing with the clay at the back of the classroom. The deal was I'd get £2 for 6 weeks, £1 at the start and £1 at the end of the six weeks."

"You really are cunning aren't you. Thn.... shifty even," answered Beth, quickly sidestepping a lisp.

"Deal is over now," mumbled Barnaby turning sideways, forming a hidden fist with his right hand. "I haven't got it. Ma needed it for something important."

"You owe me 2 weeks sling time. Where is it Spruddge? Can't back down on a deal. Everybody knows that." screamed Rivett, also turning sideways to hide a fist.

"Well, you can't have what I haven't got, but you can have this instead," shouted Barnaby as his punch flew forward in a championship wining right hook. Sadly, it soared straight past Rivett's left ear and any element of surprise disappeared with it.

"Missed me," screamed Rivett as his fist appeared from behind his coat, tracing the path of a beautifully formed upper-cut.

"Thwack!" It was the sound of very solid knuckles connecting with Barnaby's chin, causing him to stumble backwards towards the floor.

A tooth flew out and arched skywards.

"Oh no," yelled Barnaby, quickly gaining his balance. "I need that!"

"Thtopit !"

cried Beth, using a whole lungful of air as she bravely pushed between the boxers, stretching her arms to the full. Strangely and unexpectedly, Rivett did just that, puzzled, with his eyes almost popping from their sockets..

"What *are* you doing now?" he asked, staring at Barnaby rummaging on the floor. "What are you doing in those nettles?

"I've got to find it," shouted Barnaby on his hands and knees. "Got to. It's important," as he searched through the nettles with his bare hands. "There!" he shouted, lifting something tiny and white from the nettles, quickly placing it in his pocket, right next to the bag of white dog poo.

Rivett then turned his attention to Beth.

"What did you say?" he asked grinning his nastiest cheek to cheek grin. "Did you just say Thtopit? You got a lithp Beth Thaunders? Thaunders got a lithp. Thaunders got a lithp. Thundery Thaunders." taunted Rivett.

"Don't you dare call me that. Are you making fun of my dad?" asked Beth, as her hand formed a bunch of snow-white knuckles.

"Yes, Thundery Thaunders. Thund……"

"Whapppp!" as with one almighty swing her fist hit him smack on the nose.

"Why did you do that?" asked Rivett, groaning on the floor, wiping a river of blood from his face. "I was only having a bit of a laugh. You always take things so seriously you do."

"Thpruddgey, where are you?" asked Beth as she turned, dusting her hands. "Crumbs, look at you." she said, examining his face. "That'th going to be quite a bruithe. Look at your handth though. They're red raw. What on earth were you thinking of? What with in those nettleth anyway?"

Barnaby was still a bit dazed and bemused with all the lisping but managed to answer. "Didn't you see it? A tooth. Not losing than now am I. Cash in hand that is."

Beth held Barnaby's hands up to his face. "You were prepared to thuffer like this just for a tooth?"

Barnaby nodded and whispered, "Posh girl……you'll never understand."

"Quick." snapped Beth, turning towards the school door. "The bell will be ringing in a minute. You know what Old Forty's like if we don't get to the door on time."

"Aaaaaugh," moaned Rivett, sounding just like a rusty gate hinge.

"Get up," stated Beth as she encouraged him to his feet with a hard tug on the shoulder of his jacket. "You really are a bit of a softy deep inside aren't you Rivett. I didn't hit you that hard. And don't worry, nobody saw it happen and I won't tell a living soul. No point really. Nobody would believe me anyway. Don't you ever dare call me 'Thundery' though. " She turned and winked at Barnaby, then whispered, "Never underestimate the power of a posh girl. Never."

All three children were in the same class at school. Mr. Fortitude Jones' class, the deputy headmaster and a poorer teacher you'd have to search long and hard to find. He'd started his career at a time just after the war, when the country needed lots of teachers. Ex-soldiers had been trained as teachers in lightning quick time. Some had proved to be great at the job but not Mr. Fortitude Jones. In all honesty, he'd should have stayed in the army, standing guard duty in the North African desert. He often told stories of his old army days and the children would encourage him and goad him onwards as it meant that they didn't have to work. They'd sailed with him on his sea voyage around Cape Town, then North to the Red Sea eating tinned mangos along the way. He had shared his pictures of the pyramids and the Sphynx. They all managed to get into the cabin of his lorry, bumping its way across Egypt, cooking eggs and corned beef on the top of the engine housing. By the time Friday afternoon came around it was all he could do to stay awake no matter how much noise the class created. He did have one good point though. He loved taking the children on outings and trips. Some people said that he was fond of taking trips because his brother owned the coach company and he was just doing his best for the family business. On this particular day, Barnaby payed more attention than usual when *Old Forty* announced the reason for the latest outing.

"Pay attention now everybody, yes everybody. You too Nigel Rivett..... What's happened to your face.....Spruddge? You need to listen to this too boy...good grief, look at your hands....get them washed playtime...Beth Saunders, stop smirking....now. Pay attention. Everybody sit uppppppp. NOW. I've planned a little trip for next Friday.

We have to learn something about education and business partnerships this term."

"What's that all about then Sir?" queried Beth.

"Well, we have to look at some of the local businesses and factories so that you can be better informed about the sort of jobs that you'd like when you leave school. You also need to learn how businesses actually make money." Old Forty announced positively.

"Oh no," gasped Barnaby.

"Aaaaaugh," as Rivett's rusty gate opened again.

In fact, a collective gasp of dread and horror spread around the room and children started quickly thinking of a believable excuse not to go.

"No Sir, Not the glove factory again is it Sir?" shouted Rivett.

" No no, not the glove factory. No, not after what happened last time. No, not the glove factory." assured Old Forty.

Like a Mexican wave, a sigh of relief passed around the class.

"Where then Mr. Jones?" questioned Beth. She thought it wise not to attempt to say 'Sir'. Not in front of the whole class. Sir was really lisp unfriendly.

"I've organised a trip to The Splendid Snooker Balls Storehouse down in Faith, at the bottom of the valley," said Mr. Fortitude Jones. His chest pumped out with pride because he knew how hard it was to get a visit to this particular factory."

Rivett appeared overjoyed, "The new place, where they make tournament snooker balls?" he inquired with real enthusiasm.

"Of course." shouted Jones, "although I've been told that they make a few other items as well. They make piano keys and just recently they've started making bowling balls."

Barnaby had listen to all of this new information, quietly taking everything in. Normally, he'd be quite embarrassed whenever there was a trip. Ma Spruddge could never find the money, meaning that Barnaby always had to make up excuses about not being able to pay. This trip was going to be different though. He still had two unspent pounds from the sling deal. Last week, he'd received ten pence tooth fairy money. Also, there was the promise of more money from delivering Mr. Simpkins' rats to their doom. All in all, Barnaby felt rather flush. Minted in fact.

Maybe he'd treat himself to this trip. At the very least, he'd spend a bit more time near Beth. He gently raised his still very sore, nettle covered hand.

"Yes, what is it Spruddge. You've got something else on that day I suppose." smirked Mr. Jones.

"Oh no Sir," replied Barnaby. "I was just wondering Sir, how much will it cost?"

"One pound," replied Jones, "and try to get it in on time if you please."

One pound. Barnaby smiled. He could easily afford that. He raised himself from his seat and walked towards the teacher's desk. Taking his money from his pocket, he counted out two fifty pence coins. That left him with a a few dull and grimy ten pence coins, the ones left over from the sling deal. One coin though shone like silver on a sunny day. That was his fairy coin. He slipped that coin and one other back into his pocket and paid for the trip with the two grimy fifty pence coins – handing them over proudly to Mr. Jones. He in turn looked totally amazed. He'd never managed to get any trip money from Spruddge before.

"There you go Sir." said Barnaby. "You write that down in your cashbook if you please Sir. I'll make sure I get a letter to say that I can go. I'll make sure Ma signs it with her best joined up writing Sir." and with a tiny nod of his head he turned and walked back to his seat. It had been worth a pound just to see the look on Jones' face – sheer astonishment.

Playtime slowly came around, like watching sand pass through an egg timer. Beth figured out that the school day was by then one quarter over. Barnaby had run his hands under the cold tap on several occasions. His nettle rash felt a little better but still stung like the blazes. He had walked from the outside toilets into the yard when yet once again, Rivett confronted him, appearing right in front of his face.

"What now?" asked Barnaby.

"I saw what you were after in those nettles," chuckled Rivett. "I knocked a tooth out didn't I? You OK?"

"Yes, I am OK, no thanks to you though and anyway, what's it to you?"

"Got to look after one of my loyal customers haven't I. Not going to let one small problem get between us, am I. Anyway, out of interest, where is that sling?"

"Ma needed it," explained Barnaby. "She stuffed it into a rat hole."

"Uuurgh," gulped Rivett. "I hate rats. Look at your hands though. You did all that for a tooth. Why?"

"Money in the bank isn't it. Ten pence in my pocket and its MY ten pence. You know the Fairy Rule. Nobody can take that money from me. That's my money. That's why I wanted it so bad."

"Ten pence?" queried Rivett.

"Yes, ten pence. My Fairy money. I'll have it in my pocket tomorrow morning."

Neither had realised that Beth had caught up with them. Barnaby hoped she hadn't here'd the conversation about the rat hole and the sling. She looked at him quizzically. "Only ten pence?" she whispered. "We get fifty penth for a tooth in my part of the town."

Rivett nodded in complete agreement for once with Beth. "Me too. Fifty pence for a tooth. I thought everybody had fifty pence for a tooth." Rivett reached out and grabbed a small boy who happened to be passing by the shoulder. Barnaby didn't know him by name but knew that he came from his part of town and lived near the rat farm.

Straight away, Rivett saw the germ of a business opportunity begin to emerge. "Hey, my little friend, I was just wondering how much money do you get from the tooth fairy?" he questioned.

The tiny boy looked surprised and startled. He was sure that Rivett wasn't actually his friend – what had his mother told him about strangers? He spluttered his answer as quickly as he could, "Ten pence a tooth. Just like everybody else. Why do you ask?"

Rivett dropped him like a hot potato then raced around the playground asking the same question to a few other children from

Barnaby's part of town. He came back beaming, shaking his head and whispering, "Well fancy that. A clear price difference for teeth. Who'd have thought." He thought for a moment, smiled and then turned to Barnaby.

"So, here's the deal," whispered Rivett. "You give me that tooth. I take it home tonight, put it under *my* pillow and tomorrow I'll give you twenty five pence."

Barnaby pointed out to Rivett that tomorrow was indeed Saturday – also giving himself some much needed thinking time before responding to the 'deal'.

"OK then, I'll give you twenty five pence first thing Monday morning." Rivett added in an excited voice.

Barnaby snorted...."AND you'll keep twenty five pence."

"Well, a deal's a deal. Got to be something in it for me hasn't there. I've got overheads you know. After all, I'll be honest, my comic club isn't as profitable as it ought to be," responded Rivett.

Beth, who originally been on the outside of the main discussion started showing more than a passing interest in this idea. "Just two questions here. Do you honestly think this will work and how does Spruddgey know that you'll pay up?"

Rivett stared straight into Barnaby's eyes. "I'll make The Promise to you right here and now. The Sealed Promise."

Beth and Barnaby's faces broke into a knowing smile. Everybody at Hope Primary knew that you simply couldn't break The Sealed Promise. Those who did; and there were so very very few, had the name 'Breaker' added before their name. It meant that from that day on nobody ever believed a single word that you said. The name even stuck with you after school. You could only escape that name by moving away from the district. If you lived in the wrong part of Hope town, then that was probably a good thing anyway but believe me, nobody ever wanted to be known as Breaker.

"Quick Beth. Seal The Promise before he changes his mind," whispered Barnaby.

The two boys shook hands, then clutched hands together. Beth placed her hands over the boys' clenched fists. Some other nearby children saw what was happening and quickly formed a rough circle of witnesses around the three.

"Say the words," whispered Rivett.

"I promise to give you my tooth." Barnaby spoke the words not with his normal shyness but with complete confidence. He'd never been involved in The Promise before and he wanted to make it right.

"It will will never work. Not in a million years." whispered Beth.

"Ssshh." whispered the two boys.

"And I promise to take your tooth, put it under my pillow, collect the Tooth Fairy money and Monday morning give you twenty five pence."

"And keep the other twenty five pence." Barnaby finished through clenched teeth.

"Barmy……totally barmy…..the two of you." declared Beth Suddenly, her voice lifted and she boomed out. "Thay the words of The Promise." Her voice carried the length and breadth of the whole playground and surprised and hushed children and turned to look and listen. The three of them chanted as one,

"This Promise that is spoken means this Promise can't be broken."

As the words were chanted, all four hands raised and fell with the rhythm of the rhyme. Then the two boys using their left hands actually also came together in a high five. All at once, the whole playground erupted with the chant,

"This Promise that is spoken means this Promise can't be broken." and everybody started clapping. Most of the children present remained clueless as to what the promise was. They'd find out later. The playground gossip spread through Hope Primary like the nettle rash had on Barnaby's hand, and almost as fast as the smell from the glove factory on a hot day in July. The one thing that they all knew though was that

The Sealed Promise had been made and that The Sealed Promise would be kept.

CHAPTER 4.

The Final Journey of Waldo and Horace?

It was extremely hard for Barnaby to come to a final decision. Would it have been better for him personally if this normal Saturday had actually turned out to be a school day? Would it, he pondered be any better to actually spend hours sat withering in Mr. Fortitude Jones' classroom multiplying numbers that probably didn't need to be multiplied? On the other hand, would he have preferred to spend time pointlessly writing out imaginary menus, pointless instructions or mock interviews. Would his life have significantly been improved by spending the day near Nigel Rivett, even if Rivett did owe him some money? Mind you, a few hours in the company of super sophisticated Beth Saunders might have just tipped the balance and resulted in a clear cut decision. Instead, he'd have to spend some time in the not so chirpy company of Waldo and Horace, unbeknown to them, two soon to be lab rats and probably soon to be no more.

He sat there, in the deserted weather beaten bus shelter, just simply thinking. Lost in his daydream, he remembered the oddities that occurred around his porridge and later at the rat farm. Something very strange indeed had happened that morning. Old Ma Spruddge had asked him why he was up so early on a Saturday. He'd carefully explained his mission to her and that he was doing a real favour for Mr. Simpkins the Rat Man. She had actually been quite nice to him on this particular morning. Good moods for Ma were scarce events since dad had left them. Initially he couldn't quite understand why the unusual change in heart, but then he remembered her delight when he'd handed over the bag of white dog poo. His treasure from yesterday's journey to school had made Ma's eyes light up with joy – something he hadn't seen for a very long time.

"Oh my word!" she had exclaimed. "So you're not so useless after all. Well done indeed young fellow-me-lad. Maybe you will have a breakfast egg this Sunday. A bag of white. A real rarity. Well done indeed."

"Mr. Simpkins asked me to take a couple of his rats down to the laboratory. Shouldn't take long Ma. I'll take the bus. Should be back in an hour or so." Barnaby had reassuringly explained.

"You seeing Simpkins?" Ma asked strangely, and for once she didn't shout. Instead, a strange momentary twinkle appeared in her eyes.

"Yes," he answered. "Promised to put something in my pocket too."

All at once, Ma raced to the door. "You wait there!" she shouted, turning her head quickly in his direction. In fact, she turned so quickly, she lost her balance and banged into the door post – shoulder first, followed by her head. After dusting herself down and soothing her bruised forehead with the back of her right hand she repeated, "Wait there. I'll be back in a jiffy." Despite still being all a dither, she was back in a jiffy too. Hardly a minute had passed when she burst through the door carrying a small white paper bag. Passing it to Barnaby she asked him, "Give this to Simpkins please. Tell him it's from me."

Barnaby nodded to himself, thinking the whole event as being very strange. He honestly couldn't remember the last time that old Ma Spruddge had used the word 'Please'.

He finished the last dregs of his salty porridge, grabbed his coat and scarf off the hook on the back of the kitchen door and walked out into a cold frosty morning. Things became even stranger when he peeped inside the small white paper bag. There inside, was a large, warm, brown chocolate eclair, fresh that morning he guessed from Mr. Lewis' bakery at the end of their street. Strange indeed – very, very strange.

Still daydreaming, he remembered that it took effort to rouse Mr. Simpkins from a deep sleep that morning. In fact, Barnaby was about to turn and leave when the door flew open. There he was, wrapped in an old woollen dressing gown, hair bedraggled and uncombed and displaying a few loose feathers that had obviously escaped from a leaky pillow during the night.

"Morning young Spruddge. So good to see you and ready for your mission too I see. Ready and waiting." He gave Barnaby a wink and tapped the side of his nose as if to give the Saturday morning job an air of undercover secrecy.

Barnaby held up the white paper bag, "Ma said I should give you this." and he pushed it towards Simpkins' gnarled and withered hand.

He took it off Barnaby with a grin and immediately peered inside. A broad smile spread across his face showing off his two remaining front teeth to their full glory.

"This off your Ma?" he questioned.

Barnaby nodded in confirmation.

"Why'd she send this to me?" he queried.

"Honestly Mr. Simpkins, I have no idea," replied Barnaby in complete and utter honesty.

Simpkins took another look inside the bag. "Perfect," he whispered. "Just perfect for my central eating?"

"Pardon?" asked the lad. "I didn't know you had central heating in your shed."

Simpkins laughed. A strange sort of laugh resembling a creaky gate and seemed to involve his whole body. "No," he nodded, "Not central heating. Central eating. It's what I do with my teeth." He pointed a grimy unkempt finger at his remaining teeth. "Central eating, because I can only really chew in the middle of my mouth you see."

Barnaby laughed out loud although to be really honest, he didn't find it a very funny joke. Simpkins turned and stepped just inside the door. He swiftly returned with what appeared to be an old dust coated wooden and wire cage. Barnaby immediately noticed two tiny pink noses and a set of whiskers protruding through the wire front of the cage – busily sniffing out their new location. Simpkins placed the cage at Barnaby's feet, and then reached into the small paper bag again. He broke two morsels from the end of the eclair then gave a piece to each rat. As if giving some reassurance he spoke to the two rats, "There you go Waldo. Horace, you too. You'll enjoy that. Now, you two boys be good whilst this nice young lad here takes you on a little trip. Make sure you behave yourselves and don't try to escape."

Simpkins then took what could only be described as a two fanged bite from the eclair. Barnaby thought he'd seen some horrible things in his time but watching this small, ratty faced man chewing on a piece of eclair with his two remaining teeth defied description and literally nearly turned his stomach.

"You be sure to give your Ma a big thank you from Old Jem Simpkins now lad. Tell her chocolate eclairs is just the right thing for my central eating. Nice and soft and not too chewy. Tell her Waldo and Horace thank her too, don't you boys." and he turned towards the cage to give their noses a final little affectionate rub. "There you go boys. Go now," he whispered as a solitary tear fell silently from the corner his right eye.

"You are NOT taking THOSE on THIS BUS now are you?"

Barnaby abruptly awoke from his daydream. A very large lady towered in front of him – nearly placing him in complete semi shadow. Her umbrella was pointing directly at Waldo and Horace who were now quivering with fright at the back of their cage. Barnaby was pretty sure that it was Waldo who had actually started squealing as if in pain – no doubt, brought on by real fear. She raised her gloved hand toward Barnaby's face. Her finger pointed directly between his eyes. "You are not bringing those onto a bus….not any bus that I'm catching. Now take that filth and your own filth and get away with you." Following her outburst, the bus actually arrived - pulling up noisily at the bus stop. The woman stepped onto the bus, then turned quickly to block any attempt by Barnaby to follow and get onboard. By slightly turning her face, but at the same time retaining Barnaby in her sight she shouted, "Drive on driver. He's trying to get on with a pair of rats. Trying to get rats onto my bus. Can you believe the cheek?"

"Not getting on my bus with those rats. Certainly not. Not with rats." shouted the driver.

Barnaby couldn't believe what had just happened – the bus had actually moved off with the woman still hanging off the platform and still angrily shaking her umbrella at him. Once more he heard her shout, "Filth. Total filth." On reflection he could never be sure whether she had actually spat at him on purpose or whether it was just the spittle flying out of her very wide mouth with the force of her feelings. Thankfully the white spray had missed Barnaby but had landed on the top of the cage – giving it a dappled effect. He watched the bus shrinking away in the distance, placed the cage on the floor and then took a small piece of newspaper from the gutter to wipe the unsavoury mess off it.

"Right me lads, we'd better start walking then." His two new friends had calmed down a little now but still jumped a mile when the cage was lifted off the floor. "Off we go now. Not far really." Through clenched teeth Barnaby whispered, "Not far. Only two miles. Won't take us long." A droplet of rain landed squarely on Barnaby's nose and a few more began to noisily hit the side of the bus stop. "Won't take long. Not far." he repeated to nobody in particular except himself and the rats.

The walk took the best part of an hour. By the time Barnaby and the rats had reached their final destination, he was cold, wet and thoroughly miserable. Mostly miserable if the truth be told as he felt completely dejected. It had been an easy walk, pretty much a straight road all the way but the rain had seeped right through his coat, soaking him to the skin. He spotted a piece of pie crust lying on the grass beside the gutter. Carefully placing the cage on the floor, he took the crust and broke it into two pieces.

"There you go boys. A nice tasty treat for you," he said as he pushed the morsels into the cage. "No need for us all to be miserable hey." Watching Horace and Waldo tuck into their treat, Barnaby took a small, dirty rag from his pocket. "There, you enjoyed that didn't you," he said, wiping a tear from his eye and a dribble from his nose. Taking the cage again, he continued his walk.

Unfortunately, the last part of the journey was even less straightforward. A flight of steep steps about a hundred metres long defined the journey's end. By the time he reached the top he was not only panting and out of breath but perspiring heavily with steam rising from his soaking wet coat. Even his favourite scarf was no longer actually helping to keep him warm but at least it did appear to be stopping the major drips from falling down his back. At the top of the steps, he turned a corner and thankfully saw the doorway that he needed to locate. Above it hung a sign.

"Dai's Dissections. Scientific Finder of Facts"

The whole exterior of the place conveyed an air of gloom and despair. It really put the frighteners on Barnaby. As for the rats, they just sat there in the corner of the cage quietly making a sort of mewing noise. They appeared to be shaking with fear – sensing the apparent coldness of the place. Their whiskers were actually vibrating much like the string on a fiddle. Barnaby rung the bell half expecting to hear a cheery "Bbbbbbring" or maybe a happy little "Bing bong" but no. Instead, he got this:-

The unexpected response frightened the life out of Barnaby and just like the rats, he started quivering too. Strangely, despite his discomfort he recognised the tune. His teacher, often played classical music to them, "To broaden your horizons," he'd say. Barnaby recognised the response from the bell as something by a composer called Bach. Sir had told everybody that they often played the piece of music in horror movies.

The door opened. Unsuddenly. Unswiftly. Un-lickety-split . In fact, Barnaby couldn't ever remember a door opening so slowly in his whole life. To make matters worse, it also made a loud, shrill, nerve tingling creaking sound as it did so.

"SKKKKKRRRRRREEEEEEEEEEEEEEEEEEEEEEEEEEEEEEEK. " went the door.

"EEEEEEEEEEEEEEEEEEEEEEEEEEEEEEEEEEEEEEEEK" went Waldo and Horace in response.

Barnaby just stood there, trembling, knees knocking, turning a paler shade of grey. After what appeared to be a lifetime of waiting, a man appeared in the small gap created by the partly opened door. He was very short, bald and badly needed a shave. He was so short, that he actually had to look upwards to catch Barnaby's eyes.

"Yes?" he said with a deep, booming voice - a voice that just didn't match the stature of the man. "Yes," he boomed again." What do you want?"

"I've.......um.. brought you two rats. Two rats Sir. Waldo and Horace," muttered Barnaby, his feet shuffling anxiously.

"Beg your pardon?" The stranger's voice boomed out again. Barnaby managed to detect a Welsh accent. It was like looking at a poodle but hearing a blood hound.

"Rats from Mr. Simpkins up in Hope Town. He asked me to bring them to you. Sorry, I didn't quite catch your name," responded Barnaby more confidently.

"No, well you wouldn't have now would you. You wouldn't have because I never told you did I now. It's Dai. Dai Dissections. Dai, the Scientific Guy. Now what about these rats?" bellowed Dai but at a slightly lower volume compared to his initial greetings.

"Two rats for you from Mr. Simpkins," responded Barnaby.

"Oh, you haven't gone and brought me more rats have you. I wrote to him to cancel the order. Told him I did. I'm full up with rats I am. Ratted out so to speak. Over ratted. You'll have to take them back now won't you," Dai replied bluntly and very matter of fact.

Barnaby's face must have shown his feelings. He'd have to walk back in the rain now as he was pretty sure he wouldn't get onto the bus with a cage of rats. If the woman who he'd encountered at the bus stop this morning wasn't catching the return bus then some other woman with rat-phobia would be.

"Don't look so gloomy now lad. Don't look so glum. I know your problem. You don't want to go back to Simpkins without the rat money. Now, I don't want to upset him do I. I'll need more rats from him someday. Don't want to ruin our relationship now do I. Indeed to goodness, no I don't. Tell you what, you wait there and I'll be back in a flash," explained Dai in a more reassuring tone. Without warning, he appeared to disappear into the depths of the building. He just vanished, then just as suddenly, there was a bright flash of light and he was back again. Barnaby was actually waiting for the door-bell to do something like "Ta Daa" when Dai held out his hand towards him.

"There you go now. Two pounds. One for Simpkins and one for you for all your trouble. OK now? No problems with Mr. Simpkins now off you go," Dai said in finality, before once again vanishing as the door slowly but noisily creaked closed.

Barnaby opened his hand. As it unfolded he found three fifty pence and five ten pence coins, lying there in the palm of his hand. The coins were a bit grimy to say the least. Some would say a bit rusty but there they were. Two perfectly spendable pounds. Barnaby's immediate thoughts then turned to the journey home, "Off we go then lads. Not far." Once again through clenched teeth Barnaby whispered, "Not far. Only two miles. Won't take........... long." Without any warning, as he turned to start the journey home, a cunning plan began to hatch in Barnaby's head.

He now indeed had the money for 'delivering' Waldo and Horace.

He could hand over that money to Mr. Simpkins.

Mr. Simpkins need never ever know that Dai Dissection didn't actually need the rats – did he.

Barnaby knew a place near the laboratory. There was a little stream with trees and gorse bushes all around. Barnaby often went there at autumn time because nuts and blackberries could be gathered from the hedgerows providing him and Ma Spruddge with a little extra to add to their porridge. It was always worth taking a trip down here in early September, not just because of the harvest but it really was a charming place to visit. "It would be perfect," thought Barnaby. "Just perfect. The perfect place for two rats."

He squeezed himself between two hazelnut trees then wriggled past a thorn bush. Trying not to slip on the muddy bank of the little stream, he carefully placed his cage down on a patch of wet grass. Waldo and Horace gazed at him in complete bewilderment through the wires of the cage, not quite knowing what to expect next.

"You two deserve some freedom," whispered Barnaby. "Even rats deserve a favour sometimes," he said to justify what he was about to do next. Barnaby reached forward to untwist the piece of wire that kept the cage closed - opening its door. The two creatures initially cowered away but then turned and stared at Barnaby. At first, they didn't know what to do. They both turned their heads slightly, giving the lad a final quizzical look, before swiftly bursting out of the cage and heading at great speed towards the stream.

It took the two rats a while to enjoy their new found freedom. They went rummaging around their new surroundings, as rats do, and just besides a flat moss covered rock, Horace found something. It was a nut that had probably been left from the autumn fruit harvest or possibly from somebody's Christmas stocking. He sat himself up on his haunches and started enjoying his treat having successfully cracked open the nut, when Waldo reappeared. Waldo made a quick series of 'hurry up' gestures and noises as if to say, "Come quick before he changes in mind." Horace was in no rush though. He was in fact a very trusting sort of rat. He finished his lucky find, enjoying every last fragment. Then in double quick time, they both scampered from the scene - just like rats up a drainpipe some might say.

Barnaby did however manage to get the bus home although the rat cage did earn him some funny looks. He got off the bus at The Morgue and ambled down to the rat farm. Simpkins was stood outside on his front step, gazing around looking as though he'd lost something.

"Oh, there you are young Spruddge. Glad to see you back. So good of you. Everything OK?" uttered Simpkins inquisitively.

"Have you lost something?" asked Barnaby?

"Yes, I have. How did you know that? You can see into the future can't you? Psychic you are. Tell me, what's your star-sign? Taurus I bet, or maybe Pisces? No, it's Elspeth actually. Elspeth's gone missing she's my best female breeding rat. Good rat is Elspeth. She's probably escaped, trying to find Waldo and Horace. Very fond of Waldo and Horace she was. Oh, is that their cage?" uttered Simpkins without even taking a second breath.

Barnaby simply answered to the flood of information with a nod.

Simpkins grabbed the cage. He opened the front and peered inside. He saw something deep within its depths caught in the bottom right corner. Using his boney, gnarled finger and a grimy twisted nail, he wheedled it out carefully. He held it up to the sunlight as though he'd found a piece of valuable treasure. It was a tiny piece of chocolate eclair, a piece that the rats had surprisingly left behind.

"Yummy." Simpkins exclaimed as he popped the morsel into his mouth. "Uurgh," exclaimed Barnaby, quickly trying to stifle his shock. What sort of person would actually eat food from a cage inhabited by rats pondered Barnaby? To Barnaby's continued disbelief Simpkins whispered, "Now, just watch this." He then carefully placed the cage on the floor with the front door open. "Ssssshhhhh now," he whispered, placing a wagging finger in front of his remaining teeth. "Elspeth will soon catch the scent."

After a minute or two, as if from nowhere, what appeared to be a very inquisitive rat appeared. It initially sniffed the surrounding air, and then walked cautiously towards the cage itself. It lingered for quite a few moments sniffing at the door of the cage and then quietly stepped inside. Immediately after this, Simpkins put his foot to the cage door and kicked it shut. He picked the entire cage up and was about to turn to add it to his rat collection when Barnaby coughed.

"Something for you Mr. Simpkins. Something from Dai Destruction," he added nervously.

"Dai Dissection," corrected Simpkins abruptly.

"Whatever," agreed Barnaby.

Barnaby then felt inside his pocket gathering and counted out a fifty pence and five ten pence coins. He handed them over to Simpkins and hurriedly bade him farewell. It really was a crying shame that he had actually looked closely and inspected each of the ten pence coins. If he had looked at them closely it would have been pretty obvious that one of them was different from the rest. Four were dingy and dirty looking as though they had been through the hands and pockets of a nation of coal miners and dockers. In contrast the fifth was far brighter and more silver in colour . Indeed, it looked like it had come from a fairytale castle; one that stood beside a magical blue lake surrounded by apple and cherry blossom trees, which indeed it had.

CHAPTER 5.

It was the fairies that did it.

"Glum, glum, glum."

Glum indeed.

Bleakness wasn't just the feeling inside Barnaby's heart and soul on this Sunday morning. His sullen mood accompanied the sorrowful sound that his dirty, dingy spoon appeared to be making as it slowly moved his salty porridge around the cracked bowl.

"Glum, glum, glum ……….. glum a glum glum." It was genuinely more interesting to watch the oaty mess swirl around his bowl, watching it make white, watery whirlpools than actually eating the disgusting mixture. Barnaby slowly took a spoonful and ran it around the inside of his mouth. He discovered that with just a little practice, he could squirt it in a controlled manner through his recently appeared tooth gap. "Glum, glum, glum ……….. squirty, squirty glum glum."

Wow. For once he had something really good going on here. Quite an interesting rhythm was actually emerging. Now was there anything else that he could build into the odd routine? He looked around hopefully at the mostly bare kitchen table and his eyes also soon confirmed the lack of objects and warmth in the rest of the kitchen. It was indeed very Old Mother Hubbard in design. Polite visitors might call it 'minimalist' which was actually just a nice way of saying empty. Apart from his bowl and spoon, there was nothing else on the table except for another small spoon. Still stirring and rehearsing his squirting he reached across the table and took the small spoon. Near his bowl there were five or six grooves cut into the wood. Ma used to slice bread just there and often her knife would slip and notch a groove in

that's what I'd like to know. Besides, you still got that Fairy Silver of yours? Rolling in cash you are. What if they burgled us and took that? Or have you frittered it away on comics or that posh girl up the top end? You wouldn't want your Fairy Silver burgled now would you?" ranted Ma loudly.

"Ma, I've still got my ten pence. Haven't spent it yet. It's here in my pocket." He reached into his pocket, fumbled around amongst the dust and the fluff and found the coin. Quickly, he took it out and proudly placed it near the centre of the table. Taking his hand away, they both stared at it - a dirty, dark, oily ten pence coin - and it was now the centre of their attention.

Complete and utter silence engulfed the entire room.

They both stared at the filthy coin. Both looked completely puzzled.

"THATSSNOTNOFAIRYSILVERTHATSNOT." screeched ma. "Fairy Silver are always shiny and gleamy. Everybody knows Fairy Silver is shiny and gleamy. That silver looks like its come from the bottom of the spruddging tank. Where did you get that?" she inquired.

Like a human calculator sums started surging through Barnaby's brain.

He'd started the week with one pound from the infamous sling deal. Then, the other night, after losing a tooth, he'd got his Fairy Silver, ten pence. That made one pound ten pence altogether. One pound had gone to Mr. Jones for the Snooker Ball factory trip. That still left him with ten pence. Add to that the two pounds from Dai Dissections and that made a total of two pound ten pence. "Two pound ten pence." thought Barnaby. " I've never ever had that much money before." Returning his mind back quickly to the sum he also remembered getting two pounds for Waldo and Horace and giving a pound to Mr. Simpkins. Taking into account the one manky coin on the table, then there must still be more cash in his pocket. He reached deep inside, delved even more deeply into the fluff and dust at the bottom and was relieved to find some more coins. He took them and placed them next to the other on the table.

Complete silence was once again the order of the day in the room. Filthy, dirty coins sat in a dusty cluster on the table.

"WHEREDJAGETSOMUCHMONEY? You been a-thieving? And look at them. Stinking they are." Ma shouted, breaking the extended silence.

"No." Barnaby answered indignantly, before carefully sidling his body between Ma and the rolling pin. "Sit down and I'll explain everything."

So he did. He carefully told her all about the sling deal and the Snooker Ball factory trip and the rat delivery deal. He even tore a piece of paper from his homework book to explain the maths.

"So where has the Fairy Silver gone then?" questioned Ma.

"I must have given it to Mr. Simpkins by mistake." he replied.

"What did you get in return," Ma nervously asked.

"Nothing Ma. I owed it to him from the money Dai Dissections gave me." Barnaby responded.

"Let me get this right. You gave it to Mr. Simpkins? Old Jem Simpkins? Mr. Simpkins the Rat Man and got nothing in return. Oh, woe is me. The poor man. He doesn't deserve that. " Ma concluded, with a tear rolling down her cheek.

"Ma, what's the matter? It's only money." declared Barnaby.

"Only money says you. Don't you understand? Didn't I explain it to you? The Fairy Silver must be spent by the child, for the benefit of the child and nobody else. Don't you remember the rhyme that I told you?" Ma responded in exasperation.

"Yes I do," replied Barnaby. "But it only mentioned not giving the money to a mum or a dad."

"AAAAaaaaaaarrrrrgggh!" screamed Ma. "Have you no sense boy? What about the second verse?"

"There's another verse?" questioned Barnaby.

Ma turned her head towards the ceiling and recited the second verse.

"When the fairy leaves silver bold
it's for the child alone to hold.
If it's received by a grown-up person,
then their health will signif'cantly worsen."

"You can't just give it away for nothing. You have to get something in return for the silver. Something you and only you will see benefit from. Understand now? Why didn't you buy a comic? You'd have been perfectly safe with a comic."

Stumbling towards the door, she threw Barnaby's coat at him.

"Quick, put that on. Hurry now. Maybe it isn't too late." she huffed. "Remember, this is all your fault."

"My fault?" spluttered Barnaby in total disbelief.

"Yes, (whop), all (biff), your (bam) fault." responded Ma in her own special way.

Well, picture the comical sight. Old Ma Spruddge literally racing up the road as fast as her skinny legs would carry her. In her right hand, she clung onto Barnaby with a vice like grip. He in turn knew that if he didn't keep up, he'd end up being dragged face first through the grime. Verbal tellings off continued along the way although Barnaby still couldn't understand why this was such a big issue. Similarly, he couldn't understand where Ma was getting such strength, determination and energy from. She hauled him around the corner by The Morgue with such speed and ferocity that had he been a motorcar he'd have been freewheeling on two wheels. Finally coming to a screeching halt outside the gate to the rat farm Ma Spruddge and Barnaby stopped, both gasping for breath. Both were half doubled over by the gate, panting for all of their worth, when the two gallant sprinters heard a distant call.

"Help. Anybody there? Help me please somebody."

It was Simpkins' voice sounding very close yet still far away.

"Oh dear.....Help. Somebody please help."

Grabbing Barnaby by the scruff of his shoulder, Ma pushed him around the side of the rat shed along a path that he had never noticed before. Around the corner and along the side, before emerging into a back courtyard - where the two of them stood before the quaint and charming sight of a tiny stone-built bungalow. A small, well-tended garden guarded the front doorway, along with a whole regiment of garden gnomes, standing as if on military duty in two lines on parade along the edges of the garden path. Strangely enough, they all appeared to be staring directly at Barnaby. A few small brown hens clucked busily around the lawn scratching the lush green surface for worms and pieces of left over corn.

"Well, I never," thought Barnaby. "Who would have imagined that this place would be so lovely around the back?"

"Help!" Barnaby heard it again, much closer this time. It came from inside the cottage. Ma gave a knock on the door then pushed it so hard that it literally shuddered and almost came off its hinges – fortunately this confirmed that it was indeed not locked.

"Help! In here, please."

Ma Spruddge entered the dwelling first and endeavoured to find the location of the voice. On entering the living room she raced around the old wooden table and then drew back a thick red curtain that blocked another doorway. Ma quickly opened the door without any hesitation and beyond the curtain and doorway Barnaby could see into Simpkins' bedroom. There he was, lying on the bed and appearing to be in total agony, clutching his mouth in the palm of both his hands. He was dressed in pyjama bottoms with a grimy, old flannel vest covering his top half. The vest itself was covered in what looked like blood and egg stains. Then Barnaby noticed what appeared to be a rivulet of blood dribbling through his fingers and down his whiskery chin.

"They took my central eating!" yelled Mr. Simpkins.

"Have you called out the gas board?" queried old Ma Spruddge.

Looking totally exasperated, the Rat Man held his hands to his head. "No, not central heating. My central eating. My last three teeth." he shouted, pointing at his bleeding gums. "It was the fairies that did it, you mark my words. Rotten blighters. Why did they pick on me? What have I done to them anyway?"

For the first time since Ma and Barnaby had actually entered the room, Simpkins slowed down and took a deep steady breath. He took a careful look over his crooked, pointy nose. He then reached over to his bedside table and picked up his glasses. Placing them on the peak of his nose he peeped towards the end of the bed. "Good Heaven above." he gasped in astonishment. "Is that really you Sophie?" He then took off his glasses, wiped the grime off them with the corner of his blood-stained vest and replaced them in one swift movement. Squinting along his nose he gasped, "My word it is you Sophie. Sophie Spruddge. Fancy that, after all this time. And this must be young master Spruddge. Fancy that indeed. Now, what brings you both here anyway?"

"Sophie?" thought Barnaby. "It has been years and years since I've heard anybody calling Ma by her first name."

Ma gave Simpkins a knowing sort of smile then squeezed his foot gently through the blanket. "Do you have the makings of a nice cup of tea in this house?" she enquired.

Simpkins nodded with a toothless grin.

With a voice as sweet as honey Ma replied, "Right ho. Come on Barnaby. Leave this gentleman alone in his boudoir so that he can get dressed. You and me will be in the kitchen fixing up a cuppa tea. We've got a bit of a story to tell haven't we lad? A bit of real explaining."

Ma pulled the curtain across behind them before grabbing Barnaby by the shoulder as they left the room. Once secure in her grasp again she thrust her toothless face right up next to the lad's face,

"ALLYOURFAULTTHISIS," she stated with a sort of husky whisper.

"ALLYOURFAULT. Why couldn't you do something safe like buy a comic?" demanded Ma.

Having located the kitchen, she forced him down into an ancient chair that creaked ominously the minute he sat on it. Ma then started to search the room for the makings of a cuppa. The kitchen was a sparsely furnished room, and had the look that told that it didn't appear to regularly receive visitors. Besides the table and a couple of chairs, there was just a large mahogany chest of drawers. Ma rummaged deep within it but to no avail, as she only found the sock drawer initially followed by the underwear drawer. On opening the top right hand drawer a broad smile spread across her face because she came across the tea caddy and some sugar.

"Jem!" yelled Ma. "Any fresh milk?"

"In the pantry behind the curtain," replied the voice from the bedroom.

Ma pulled the curtain to one side, turned and grabbed a bottle of milk from the top shelf. For a fleeting few moments, with the corner of his eye, Barnaby caught a glimpse of the inside of the pantry. He noted some breakfast cereal, bread, a butter dish and what looked an awful lot like a bottles of ginger beer on the various shelves. Barnaby's attention was forced to return to a more important matter that caused his jaw to almost hit the floor.

BAM!! Coming suddenly back to the real world, Barnaby noticed that Ma had banged a mug down in front of him.

"DONTKNOWWHYIMGIVINGYOUTHIS" Ma stated with a harsh whisper. "Don't deserve it after what you've done. "

Shortly after this the bedroom door opened. Barnaby was stunned with the shock of what he saw framed in the open door. There stood a man, hair still wet and slicked over his slightly balding head. Clean shaven. Could Barnaby indeed detect a whiff of after shave?. He wore an Irish style collarless shirt, crisp and freshly ironed. This was finished off with a pair of checked trousers.....deep blue with a slightly larger deep purple pattern. It took Barnaby a little while to figure out that he was witnessing - Mr. Simpkins in his very Sunday best clothes.

"Oh Jem Simpkins," whimpered Ma, "You always did brush up well. Sit down and I'll pour you some tea." Turning to glare at Barnaby she glowered, "YOUGERRUPNOW. Let Mr. Simpkins sit down. He needs a seat after what he's been through. And you, you little monster, you have some explaining to do."

So it came about that Barnaby stood there with a guilty expression and a bowed head in front of Ma and Simpkins, explaining the mix up with Dai Dissections, the coins and finally the fairy silver. He held back on telling what had become of Waldo and Horace. Some secrets are best kept for another day.

"Don't worry lad. I think I'm over it now," uttered the brave Jem Simpkins. "They were no good to me anyway. My central eaters were on their last legs. 'Bout time they came out."

"Do you know what happened?" asked Barnaby?

"Shhhhh." shushed Ma, "Maybe the gentleman doesn't want to remember the true horror of his experience right now does he."

"No, it's O.K. Nothing much to remember really lad. Just went to bed as per normal. Just as I was drifting off I remember peering outside. I'm pretty sure I saw a little golden spark coming towards me from the direction of the lake but that's all I really remember. Then woke up this morning with the taste of blood running down my throat. Transfixed with terror I was at the time. Paralysed with panic. It was only through seeing your mum again that pulled me through. Fancy seeing you again after all these years." He took a tentative sip from his tea. He winced a little as the heat hit his still raw gums but also turned to Ma and smiled a little. "Nice tea. Lovely cup of tea that is. Fancy something else though? There's the makings of a breakfast in the pantry there. I could boil some eggs for us all if you like. The girls outside have been laying well these last few days." offered Simpkins.

And so it was that Barnaby Spruddge had his first egg and soldiers breakfast in quite some time. Even though he had to eat it standing up as there were only two chairs in the room, he thoroughly loved every dip and drool of this little feast. Later, after the eggs, there was even some brown toast. Barnaby having been trusted with a pile of bread and a toasting fork - in front of a roaring open fire that had initially been kindled by Simpkins. Believe me, it tasted better than anything that Barnaby had tasted in years. Butter oozed through the bread all over his fingers although he didn't permit even the tiniest dollop of marmalade to escape. Ma had by then calmed down and appeared to be enjoying the moment, probably even more than Barnaby. She turned to him and said,

"Why don't you run home now son. I'll follow you back in a few moments. Leave us two a few moments to take a walk down memory lane together."

Barnaby finished the last of his toast and walked towards the kitchen door. He paused for a moment next to the mahogany chest. There on the lid stood an old school photograph, showing a group of possibly about thirty or so children, all wearing their Sunday best. He thought he'd recognised somebody. Pointing at the photograph, he turned to his mother and asked, "Ma. Is this you in this photograph?"

"Yes," she answered. "That's me alright. Back row towards the right. The tall girl with the ribbons. And right next to me, well that's a very young Jem Simpkins."

Glancing back into the room Barnaby noticed a twinkle in his mother's eye. A genuine twinkle. Only a small one, but very definitely a twinkle. "Curious," he thought, whilst fishing and then savouring a tiny piece of egg yolk from a crevice between his tooth gap in his mouth. "Curious," he thought again as he gently pulled the front door closed behind him and stepped onto the pathway.

It was only then that he really noticed them. The two rows of gnomes. When he and old Ma Spruddge had first walked up the path he was sure that they were all turned outwards and were staring at them. Now, as he left the house and walked back along the path, they were all looking inwards towards the house and staring directly at him again. Standing, staring deeply, with searching eyes.

"No, that's not curious," thought Barnaby. "That's just plain spooky. That just can't be right. Now pull yourself together young Spruddge."

CHAPTER 6.

Payday.

So it was, on that eventful Monday morning Barnaby walked his usual weary route to his dreary school. Something really strange had happened at breakfast time though. Something that had indeed made the boring morning breakfast ritual unusually pleasant.

"Where on Earth did that come from?" asked Barnaby, his eyes almost popping gazing at an egg. A golden brown egg. One that looked like it had come from a very plump, happy hen. "How did you manage to get that?" he asked Ma but she simply turned towards him, winked and tapped the side of her nose.

"Don't know why I'm giving you that. 'S'not like you deserves it is it. I've a feeling though that we might just be getting eggs regularly if we're lucky." was her curious parting comment as Barnaby left the breakfast table.

Leaving for school, still reflecting on the potential supply of eggs, he quickly past the morgue noticing that as usual, it was enshrouded in sullen darkness. "Nothing new going on there thankfully." thought Barnaby. Continuing along his route, he came to a sudden stop at the rat farm where Mr Simpkins halted his progress and his preoccupation with eggs.

"Morning lad. And a fine morning too. How are you now? How's your Ma? Enjoy your breakfast?" Asked Simpkins, as if in a rush to find out all the answers to his questions.

"Too many questions there," thought Barnaby, so he answered with, "Everything's just fine Mr. Simpkins," hoping that covered everything. "What are you doing?" added Barnaby deliberately in order to deflect the focus away from himself.

"Decided to clean up didn't I," came the chirpy reply. "Decided that me and the rats deserve something a little better." Simpkins was busily cleaning the stone path along the front of his farm. A pile of already gathered, partly rotted garden waste lay along one side of the forecourt, brushes and a rake leaned against the wall of the weather beaten shed. Barnaby looked the shed over carefully and noticed that the windows were actually bright and sparkling clean. Through the glass Barnaby even noticed that the rat cages were gleaming. Every cage appeared to have fresh hay lining the bottom and every single rat looked as though it had been washed and brushed as in preparation for a local show. A washing line hung to the side of the tired, rusty shack and some old but bright, white net curtains were drying in the morning sun. Barnaby had already noticed that Simpkins himself was all a-glow. Gone were the threadbare grime stained trousers literally held together with string. Instead he wore a brand new set of denim dungarees over a similarly clean checked shirt.

"Off to school hey lad?" questioned Simpkins. "Well, off you go now or you'll be late for the bell. Oh, wait a minute," he uttered and at the same time raced inside the shed. When just inside, Barnaby saw him turn a handle and open a cupboard door. Simpkins took something out, then took a few steps back out of the shed and thrust a packet of chocolate caramels into Barnaby's hand.

"There you go young-fellow-me-lad. Something for your journey to school this morning. Can't eat them myself now can I. Not since ....well, you know." Simpkins added, knowing that Barnaby already knew the reason and didn't need being told again.

It was a packet of chocolate caramels.

An egg and a packet of chocolate caramels on the same day. Barnaby couldn't believe his good fortune and pinched himself just to make sure he wasn't dreaming but everything did actually appear to be really happening. He gave Mr. Simpkins a cheery "Thank you" and waved back towards him as he raced down the lane whistling brightly, continuing his journey to school. He was just about to turn the corner when Mr. Simpkins shouted after him.

"Hey lad, give us a knock on your way home. I'll have a little something for you and your ma."

Barnaby gave him a last cheery wave and a thumbs up and immediately started wondering what the little something could possibly be.

He soon reached the familiar part of his journey where he'd have to decide whether to risk the clay pit or to take the sensible way. Strangely on this particular morning, there was no choice to be made. He'd avoid the clay pit today. He actually would have liked to have bumped into Nigel Rivett as he had a debt to collect from him. What would be the outcome of The Promise he'd negotiated with Rivett? He couldn't believe that he'd really get half of the fifty pence for just giving Rivett his tooth. In his heart he couldn't see that happening - that would simply be too good to be true – or could it happen? At the very least though, he was hopeful, expecting either ten pence or possibly just simply get his tooth back. The path turned downwards, towards the river bank; a far kinder slope than the clay pit. It actually curved downwards towards the H.G.G.L. gateway and the school gate itself. However, at first, it ran right alongside and past the Rivett household. The Rivett bungalow stood on a small, neatly kept plot of land. A well tended garden with a mock wishing well in the centre of a green lawn formed the main front feature of the plot. To the side stood a rustic looking garden shed or as Nigel Rivett affectionately called it, '*Comic Central*'. This was the place where the swopping and wheeler dealing always took place. To fit into the scheme of things the shed had large super hero posters decorating the insides. The three *Rivett Rules* were posted on the front door, rules that Barnaby to his personal painful previous experience remembered and knew so well. The rules read:

1. All who wish to make use of Comic Central must first of all provide Comic Central with 1 comic out of every ten swops. This

will be personally chosen by the manager – yours truly Nigel Rivett.

2. With regards to rule #1, there will be no arguments or discussions with regards to the chosen comic. Comic Central management decisions are final.
3. Once a swop is made, the swop becomes final. Swopped comics can only be swopped again during the next Comic Central session - when once again, rule #1 applies.

Barnaby lingered and looked, but on this particular morning there was no sign of Rivett. He thought about knocking on the door but thought better of the idea based on his previous experiences of doing so. Disappointed he finally decided to walk on towards the school instead.

As he walked through the school gate, he noticed something very unusual. The routine morning football match appeared very lack lustre with hardly any boisterous enthusiasm being shown by the players. Neither was there a skipping rope being swished round to be seen anywhere. Instead, Barnaby noticed that a group of children had formed in a circle around three others. A chant appeared to be emerging from the centre of the circle.

"The Promise that is spoken means The Promise can't be broken."

Barnaby at the same time of hearing the chant saw two hands rising to the high five. One long fingered hand belonged to Nigel Rivett. The other hand belonged to a tiny little girl from Barnaby's street. Initially he couldn't think of her name but then it came back to him. Elspeth. Elspeth Mangler. He also knew her dad, who worked down at H.G.G.L. as a mangler, somebody who runs the tanned leather through a huge mangle to squeeze out the tanning fluid.

Without warning, a voice rang out. "Spruddgey. Over here. Quick. Come and thee."

It was Beth, still lisping badly. At Beth's summons, Barnaby moved quickly towards the children, who were all by then making sort of hurry up beckoning gestures towards him. Three of the smallest in the group broke out of the circle and raced towards him. They grabbed him by the coat and scarf and literally pulled him towards the centre of the circle they'd just left.

"Pay him then," stated Beth to Rivett. "Keep your promith."

Standing at the circle's centre , Nigel Rivett didn't look particularly happy about this, but finally reluctantly reached into his pocket and pulled out a clutch of bright, shining silver coins. The sight of the coins fair nearly took Barnaby's breath away.

"Keep your promith!" stated Beth with a little more purpose and threat in her voice this time. Barnaby held out his hand in expectation.

"Ten, ten and a five. Twenty five pence" counted Rivett begrudgingly.

Beth held her heard high and shouted to the crowd, "The Promith was kept." The whole crowd, having grown significantly in number as events unfolded, burst into joyful applause.

Joyful laughter, shrill shouts and sounds of sheer happiness filled the small schoolyard - echoing out deeply in recurring waves along a small valley besides a sweet sparkling river. Happiness and hope filled the playground air as at least half of the children, the ones that scratched a life in the homes below the factory started checking their own teeth, trying to find a wiggly one. Thoughts of receiving a better deal for their teeth filled their dreams. Thoughts that maybe the potential personal wealth that they carried inside their heads had overnight, become a lot more valuable.

Once the circle of children had melted away, the usual football championship and skipping games had resumed and were back in full flow. Facts and gossip were being exchanged across the playground. Ropes were being turned and skipped over as the 'news' spread like wild fire whilst races being run along one edge of the playground carried the news to other audiences. Just two children remained glued to the spot where the circle had once formed - Beth and Barnaby.

"Have you got any idea how many promithes I'm now holding? Three already. Three. All from children living near you. That Mangler girl and the two Tanyard twins, Terry and Tony. The Promith is really taking off."

Barnaby just stood there looking at the unexpected treasure in his hand. It had really worked. It had actually worked and the outcome had outstripped all his expectations. Admittedly Rivett was now also better off but that didn't seem to matter to Barnaby. He counted the coins again. Twenty-five pence- unbelievable. Whilst placing them in his pocket, he felt something else stored in there. With all of the commotion about the fairy coins he'd forgotten his other good fortune that morning. He quickly pulled out his bag of chocolate eclairs, almost with as much bewilderment as when he'd stared at the coins. With increasing confidence he then decided that it might be the right time to do something he'd never done before. Pushing his arm forward and furiously trying to avoid blushing, he offered the bag of slightly squashed eclairs to Beth.

"Well now, you do know how to treat a girl well don't you. Always thought you were a bit of a charmer didn't I." Beth responded appreciatively as she pulled out a chocolate.

Thoughts of eggs and chocolate eclairs and fairy gold were whizzing around Barnaby's head as he returned the sweets to his pocket. On impulse though, he offered the bag again, "Take another Beth. Thanks for all your help. I owe you loads."

Looking really surprised she did take another. "I'll keep this for later," she stated, placing it carefully in her overcoat pocket. "You are, aren't you. A real charmer." she whispered. Then she looked at him fondly and winked cheekily at him.

For Barnaby the magic moment seemed to last forever but was ended by the sound of the ringing of the school bell. All the children ran to form their lines at the respective school door of entry to the building. As he lined up, Barnaby's head was still whizzing with the thoughts of all that had happened to him that morning. He reflected in a slight daze on all of the ways that his gloomy little existence had taken a clear and wondrous turn for the better.

- A breakfast egg.
- A bag of chocolate eclairs.
- A clutch of fairy silver.
- A wink from Beth Saunders – in his humble but biased opinion, the classiest girl in the whole school.

Four real treasures each worth savouring indeed Barnaby had reflected. Happy thoughts kept buzzing through his head but as he tried to place the newly acquired treasure in some sort of order of merit, there was no doubt in his mind about first place. It was that solitary wink that was the finest treasure and definitely stood at the top of the order of merit table. It had earned and taken a special place in his heart.

Worries can be dreadful things. They can find a little spot in your soul where they establish their roots and then grow and grow much like the thistles in Ma Spruddge's garden. Left untended, they'll weaken you, they'll strangle you, they'll choke you. Thankfully on his walk home, Barnaby had already decided what he would do with his latest worry. Feeling the coins in his pocket, he couldn't help but worry that somehow the normal flow of life had been turned sideways. The fairy coins started to feel like loot stolen from the bank rather than a deserved treasure. He'd have to pull his worry out by the roots and burn it. He actually remembered one of Mr. Fortitude Jones' favourite proverbs:- A problem shared is a problem halved. He'd already made his mind up, but the question was, did he have the courage of his convictions to carry things out.

The living room was unusually cold and dark when he arrived home. Ma was sat slumped in her chair besides a log fire that had almost expired. She sat there knitting what appeared to be a scarf.

"I've managed to unravel one of your dad's old jumpers. I'm knitting it into another scarf for you. I know how much you love your dad's old scarf but it's getting to look a bit old and tattered now. I'd let you have the old jumper, but you're completely the wrong shape for it. Follows after me you do....tall and lanky, not like your dad bless him." She informed him all at once.

"Ma, I've got something to show you," whispered Barnaby, changing the focus of their conversation.

"You been pinching things again?" Ma questioned. She then looked at Barnaby and noticed his face was as white as a sheet. "Lor, lummy, wha't the matter with you. Looks like you've seen a ghost."

Barnaby lowered his head and then reached inside his pocket. There in the depths, he fished out his newly acquired silver coins and carefully placed them on the table.

Silence filled the room.

"GETCHYERNOW!" screamed Ma throwing her knitting to the floor, as she jumped from the fireside. Racing around to Barnaby's side of the table, she quickly grabbed him by the throat with one forceful hand. She used the fingers of her other hand to prise open his mouth, then bent over to stare inside. Keeping his mouth open, Ma pulled him over to the window in order to get more light to shine into his mouth.

"WHEREDJAGETTHEMFROM?" she screamed at the top of her voice.

Whilst trying to keep the table between himself and the wild crazy person before him, he told her everything. Barnaby indeed blurted it all out about Nigel Rivett, the fight, the tooth, the nettles, the deal, the promise, everything. When he finally explained the part where Rivett had actually paid his debt to clear the promise, Ma just sucked in and enormous gasp of air. "Don't take your coat off," she stated. "We're going up the rat farm."

Silence was the order of the day at the Simpkins household.

Mr. Simpkins took a sip from his tea-cup.

Ma Spruddge took a sip from her tea-cup.

Barnaby somehow felt obliged to take a sip from his tea-cup. This at first inspection was indeed synchronised slurping at its very best. Looking around him, Barnaby couldn't believe the transformation that had occurred since their last visit. Everything was spotless with a luscious heavenly smell of lavender furniture polish hanging heavily in the air. The best china tea service was displayed before them, set out like chess pieces on a game board. A pile of chocolate eclairs held pride of place at the centre of the table, proudly presented on a silver platter. Potted plants flourished on every single window sill. The school photograph Barnaby had previously inspected watched over Simpkins and his guests, standing to attention on the chest of drawers and showing signs of serious recent dusting.

Sighing in collective harmony and moving as one, they all placed their tea cups back on their saucers.

Clinkclinkaclink.

"So, let me get this right," whispered Simpkins slowly stirring his tea, "You gave your tooth to another boy."

Barnaby nodded, nervously taking yet another sip of tea.

"Then he placed it under his pillow." Continued Simpkins.

Barnaby nodded again, swooshing his tea through his tooth-gap. "Squirty squirty"

"Next morning, there was twenty five pence there." Resumed Simpkins.

"No, fifty pence." Responded Barnaby matter of factly.

Simpkins almost squirted his sip of tea through his lips.

"Fifty pence" he questioned in disbelief.

"Yes, he kept half. That was his part of the deal. I got half, he kept half," stated Barnaby beginning to find some inner confidence.

"So," pondered Mr. Simpkins, "you didn't give him your fairy silver, you never had it until this boy gave it to you. You just gave him your tooth." He carefully picked up the tea pot and filled everybody's cup to the brim. Still deep in thought, he poured some of his own tea back into the tea pot to make some room for the milk. Carefully, he poured some milk into his cup, then offered the milk to his guests. "The silver that he kept, I suppose that you never really had that did you." Simpkins concluded.

"No. I've never seen it. Still haven't seen it. That went straight into his pocket," answered Barnaby reaching for the sugar bowl. He added one lump to his tea cup and was about to reach for a second when he noticed Ma giving him *the* look. Retracting his arm with one smooth movement, he proceeded to stir his tea instead.

"And no grown-ups were involved were there," chipped in old Ma Spruddge.

"Not a single one," agreed Barnaby. "Just me and Nigel Rivett."

"Can't see a problem. No, can't see any problem there, can you Sophie?" asked Simpkins.

"I don't know," she added cautiously. "Curious tale if you ask me though. Never heard of anybody getting the better of a tooth fairy before now have I. Nasty little blighters they can be. Personally I can't see any good coming of this. I certainly wouldn't try it again if you ask me."

Simpkins shook his head slowly and whilst scratching his forehead he said, "One thing you might consider trying lad. Put your money under your pillow tonight. See what happens." he told Barnaby.

"No, wait," chipped in Ma, "You're perfectly entitled to part of that cash, after all, it was your one tooth that was lost. So why don't you just put twenty pence under your pillow tonight, just to see what happens. Now, before anything else goes wrong, run up Fisher's the newsagent and buy yourself a comic. Nothing ever goes wrong with comics. Perfectly safe they are." said Ma in a resigned voice.

Barnaby waited a moment, finished his tea and concluded that Ma's idea was indeed a good one. As he rose to leave he bade Mr. Simpkins a cheery goodbye and thanked him for the tea. Turning to his mum he gave her a little wave and a nod.

"See you later Ma," he said and he walked out the door. He'd almost completely pulled it shut behind him when he heard Ma whisper to Mr. Simpkins.

"Jem, wasn't there another verse to that rhyme? A third verse to the fairy rhyme?"

In his head, Barnaby heard some familiar music. It was that piece from Bach, the one that Dai Dissection's doorbell had played.

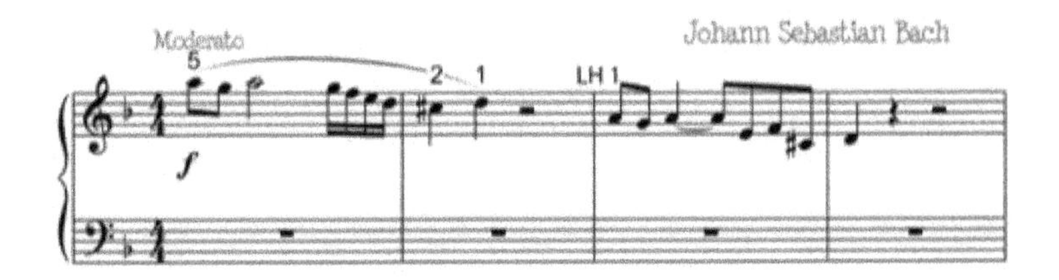

With the music from the doorbell of doom ringing through his imagination, he walked down the garden path on his way to get a comic. Once again, however, as he walked along the path he was uncomfortably convinced that each and every gnome had unbeknown to him turned in his direction. Again, they appeared to be standing to attention, fixing a stony knowing stare upon him.

CHAPTER 7.

Red, green, yellow and brown.

The week and the bleak winter continued. Normally nothing really memorable ever happens in January. Christmas lights have long been stored away. The weather continued as always dismal and damp. Even Pancake Day appears to be just a small glimmer of festive joy in the distant future. However, in a small junior school, sat besides a river that slowly meandered its way towards the factory of fashion, small subtle changes could be witnessed inside the walls and on the fences of the playground.

"Roll up, roll up, bring us your teeth. We'll do you a deal on any kind of tooth. Grinders, gnashes, bare teeth, filled teeth, brown teeth, black teeth. Just about any teeth at all," shouted Nigel Rivett with all of the skills of a market trader. "You there, Sally Squeedger, any luck with that loose tooth of yours?" A small, damp, untidy child shook her head in dismay.

"Would you like me to give it a pull?" asked Rivett, but the tiny girl just shook her head more violently.

Rivett stood besides a small flight of steps that rose towards the pathway that past the gates to the H.G.G.L. factory There was a small pillar at the end of a wall. Rivett had started to use the location as a sort of office with a make do desk.

"I've got a tooth," spoke a small voice. "Can we do the deal?" asked a small voice almost hidden under a strawberry jam caked mop of raven black hair. A yellow-stained prize was pushed across the stone surface of Rivett's desk.

"You know how this works," asked Rivett.

"I give you a tooth, we makes a promise and tomorrow you give me twenty five pence."

"Absolutely correct young man. Here's somebody with an eye for business if I've ever seen one. Now, give me your hand."

Grasping the child's hand he turned and shouted, "Beth! Got a minute?"

She turned and walked slowly towards the makeshift desk.

"I'm not going to carry any of your promises," she explained.

"I had a chat with my mother and she said that probably no good would come of it. She made me worry about how this would all end. It got me thinking. No good will come of this, you mark my words." Rivett just shook his head and carried on cornered another child.

"Rubbish. Every night, this works. I'm making a stack. You're just jealous. Nothing's going to stop this little wheeze, besides, there'll always be teeth."

Any outsider would have found it curious just watching the strange on-going business dealings. Time after time, a small child from the brown part of town would wander quite nervously over to Rivett's office. Usually they went with a friend, or a former customer of Rivett's ever growing tooth trade. A few agreement binding words would initially be quietly whispered and exchanged. Hands would then be clasped in final settlement. One of Rivett's underlings would then be summoned and *The Promise* would be made. Ivory went one way across the desk and the very next day, silver coins would be given in exchange. It was all so very odd but all so very rewarding for Rivett.

By the end of the school week, Barnaby could no longer hold his curiosity. During the afternoon break he sidled over to the tooth exchange desk. "So?" he asked inquisitively, "How's business Nigel?"

"Not so bad Spruddgey," responded Rivett, whilst continuing to trade with a young playground customer. "You must know that I'm eternally grateful to you for providing me with this exciting new business opportunity. I suppose you're now going to ask me for a cut of the action." he concluded in a sort of matter of fact way.

Barnaby shook his head in response. "No, but thanks for the offer all the same," he replied as Beth's mother's advice echoed loudly within his mind. *'No good will come of this'*. "How much trade do you get?" he asked with increasing interest, having noted the quite steady flow of interested customers.

"Well, so far, I've had at least one tooth handed in a day. I had three last Wednesday – that proved to be a real record. I'm being careful though as I only put one tooth under my pillow each night, - just in case. I also keep a list of my customers in my homework book and I put them through pillow processing in turn."

"And this all works?" asked Barnaby in increasing disbelief.

"Apparently so," responded Rivett. "Just this week I stand to make a profit of twelve pounds seventy five pence." Then as he was responding and without real warning, a tiny, grimy girl with her equally small statured and filthy friend took their place at the front of the playground counter of commerce. The first of the pair gazed up towards Rivett's nostrils and gave a small but very polite cough. Tiny specks of blood could be seen on her bottom lip but despite this clear discomfort, she wasn't crying. Neither was she upset in any shape or form. Her bravery shone through despite the pain and indeed the strange feeling she now felt in her empty gum. Deep inside her inner being, she was really looking forward to receiving the improved payment from Rivett's Tooth scheme.

Rivett turned to Barnaby and smiled, "Make that thirteen pounds Spruddgey," he whispered, before turning to deal with his newest client.

And so the playground trade in newly lost teeth flourished and established itself through the early weeks of winter. Playtimes came and went, playground goals were scored and disputed, whilst skipping ropes continued to spin – and blood stained teeth were indeed exchanged for sparkling fairy silver.

One event did, however, break the routine monotony of the dark days of winter, with the much anticipated Jones' trip to the snooker ball factory.

"Hurry up now, everybody on board. Make sure you sit with your partner. That's the one that I paired you off with in class. Remember, no singing, none of you, is that clear. After all, we don't want to keep the bus driver awake do we," bellowed Jones from the front of the bus whilst consulting his clipboard.

Barnaby actually found Jones' attempt at a joke quite funny but stopped when he finally realised that he was the only one laughing.

"Haven't you heard that one before?" asked Rivett in disbelief at Barnaby's response. It was evident that *Old Forty* cracked this same joke at the start of every trip. The only other person still laughing was the bus driver who continued to do so as he turned the engine on. Sadly, Barnaby asked himself how many trips he'd missed as he'd never heard the quip before. Previously Ma had found it impossible to find the cash and so he'd missed out repeatedly. A smile soon returned to his face though when he remembered that this particular adventure was being paid for by a fall on the clay pit, a sprained arm and a deal with the Rivett Finance Company. Looking around the bus as the class took their seats, he noticed other children from his part of town taking their seats and belting themselves in. All of them had beaming, gummy smiles on their faces looking forward to this unexpected treat – all partly financed by Fairy silver no doubt.

A while ago, Barnaby had travelled the very same route the bus was now taking on foot, carrying two rats in a cage. Today was, however, far more civilised an experience. A plush luxury coach with all the mod-cons courtesy of Mr. Jones' brother. They even drove past the flight of steps that lead to Dai Dissections scientific laboratory and in due turn the waste ground that was probably now the home to two very happy rats. A little further down the road, the bus pulled into the front courtyard of a concrete blockhouse sort of factory. Immediately, chattering with excitement, having arrived at the destination they left their seats, all trying to be the first off the bus.

"Back, back," shouted Mr. Jones, pretending to beat them into control with his rolled up newspaper. Once outside the bus and with the children all lined up ready to go, Mr. Jones stepped inside the foyer of the factory through a door marked by a sign with red lettering "All visitors report to reception please." Meanwhile, Mrs. Saunders, today's volunteer helper kept the two lines of chatty children standing firmly to attention until somebody started a song,

"The wheels on the bus go round and round,"

Beth, standing just in front of Barnaby was giving the familiar nursery rhyme her all, when she turned, stopped and gazed towards the sky. Her arm shot upwards to try to trace the path of whatever it was that caught her attention. She turned around and asked Barnaby, "Did you see that?"

"Pardon?" responded Barnaby in a confused tone.

"Did you see it? Flew towards that upstairs factory window then vanished inside." Beth declared excitedly.

"No," replied Barnaby. "What did it look like?"

"Bright shiny gold and all fluttery. Maybe a bird? Perhaps somebody's flying a kite from that window?" Beth continued breathlessly.

"No, I di........" and but then Barnaby did see something. Tiny and shiny, just as Beth had described, but this time flying out of the window and disappearing just as quickly as it had appeared.

"There, I bet you saw that. You couldn't have missed that," whispered Beth. "What was it," she asked in disbelief.

"No, I saw it," replied Barnaby. "Looked a bit like a canary if you ask me. Maybe a budgie. Flying towards Hope Town. "

"OK class." shouted *Old Forty*, "Step this way now and remember, whatever you do, don't touch anything that you shouldn't touch. Keep your hands firmly inside the barriers. Any lost limbs will be served up as tomorrow's dinner. Pay particular attention to our tour guide here, Dai"

Thoughts of the golden fluttery thing were quickly forgotten though. Barnaby was totally taken aback. It was indeed the Dai Dissections that he knew ....wearing white overalls under a bright yellow high-vis vest, a bright yellow safety helmet and Barnaby also noted he was sporting a clean shave.

"Good morning children, good morning to you all - can you hear me at the back?" Dai jovially addressed the assembled group.

Could they hear him was indeed not in doubt? When Dai spoke it was as if the very fabric of the building shook. Jaws dropped and backs straightened and expressions of pure shock spread across the young faces of an entire class of children. Nobody could believe that such a loud deep voice could come from such a small man.

"Now, if you'll all step this way," bellowed Dai, "first of all I'll take you through to the extrusion room. Keep together now, we wouldn't want to lose anybody like we did last week now would we." This last comment brought a hushed nervous silence to the whole group.

Factories are quite different places to classrooms. They lack the routine order and quiet symmetry of the school environment. Instead, everything appears to be placed in a disjointed yet purposeful muddle. Steam could be seen and heard whooshing from a pipe above a higher up balcony. Large brightly coloured glass containers lined one of the walls. They were set out in order, white, red, yellow, green, brown, blue, pink and black. For some reason, the red bottle was far larger than all of the others. Elsewhere, large pieces of machinery moved around in regular patterns, moving much like a dancer on a stage. Across the factory floor Barnaby could see two conveyer belts, each carrying what looked like toothpaste but on a very much larger scale. Two long, large toothpaste squidges were slowly moving towards a machine that appeared to cut each squidge into a regular length. Beyond all of these sights though, two other important pieces of information hit the children's senses. First, the sheer noise of the factory floor. In the background, coming from the wall behind the point where the toothpaste appeared, there came a sound. A horribly high pitched grinding sort of sound. It sounded like a high powered electronic machine, resembling a drill, or maybe some kind of grinder. A noise like no other, but at the same time sounding a bit like nails on a blackboard with the volume turned up high.

"Maybe it would have been better at the glove factory after all," mumbled Barnaby. "Still, the smell isn't so bad," he added as his nose twitched to a most peculiar odour.

Rivett sidled up to Barnaby and asked, "Hey Spruddgey. What is that smell? I'm sure I've come across it before."

Beth turned around, "Do you know, it smells just like the dentist to me."

A number of nearby children's heads having heard the conversation nodded in agreement.

Barnaby caught Dai's eye. "Scuse me, it's Dai isn't it. Dai Dissections."

"Oh now indeed to goodness, there's a familiar face if ever I saw one, now who is this then?" responded Dai to Barnaby's questioning. Even when he whispered, Dai's voice was still strong enough to curdle milk. " Oh yes- now I remember, Mr. Simpkins' delivery boy as I live and breathe. How is he now old Jem. Hope he didn't get upset when you took those rats back."

"No, he was fine about that," lied Barnaby openly in an attempt to end the conversation about the two rats he'd set free. "Tell me though, what's Dai Dissections doing here?"

"Oh, it's just a little side-line of mine you know, taking tours around this marvellous factory. Must tell you though, I'm not Dai Dissections in this factory. Here, they call me Dai Directions – I take groups round you see." giving Barnaby his usual wink as he turned away.

"How do you know him?" whispered Beth.

"Trust me," answered Barnaby, "You really wouldn't want to know the truth on that front."

"Children," boomed Dai Directions as he pointed to the on-going activity behind him. "If you could just cast your attention to these two large squidges rolling down our conveyor belt just there. Yes, I know they both look the same but here," he said, pointing repeatedly towards the farthest squidge, "Is our Class A paste. This one gets moulded into our Class A Tournament Snooker Balls. They are the very ones that get used by the top class professionals like Tornado Thomas, the current national champion. He also proudly wears the sponsorship badge of this very factory." Puffing himself up with pride, Dai Directions continued to sell the company line and pointed to a large, framed photograph of Tornado Thomas with his gleaming smile and dark rimmed glasses, holding a shining trophy in one hand and a black snooker ball in the other. The picture displayed the company caption, "The Splendid Snooker Balls Storehouse. So splendidly smooth."

Beth raised her hand, "Excuse me Dai, why are there two lines of squidges?"

Her mum, Mrs F, turned and looked proudly at her brainy daughter then whispered, "Lisp left you then Beth?" she replied noticing Beth's smile.

"Now there is a bright girl isn't she. Bright as a button you are aren't you." replied Dai, not noticing the look of parental pride showing on Mrs. Saunders face. "Bright indeed, and I'm so glad you asked that question. You see, that's our Class D paste. Now, although it looks the same, it isn't really . It's a vastly inferior product it is. You can't make tournament balls out of this muck, no. It still has its uses though. Tell me. How many of you had small sized snooker tables delivered by Santa last Christmas?"

A few hands were raised whilst most of the children gave a knowing smile thinking of Santa trying to deliver a snooker table down a chimney.

"Well, you'll notice, the balls are much smaller. They don't have to take the same amount of pressure as a competition ball. No, indeed they don't. So because they don't take the big hits that the professionals can give in a competition, it's perfectly safe to use D paste for small table balls." Explained Dai as if sharing some national secrets.

"Safe?" asked Barnaby.

"Yes, safe." boomed Dai.

"What do you mean by safe?" asked Barnaby again.

Dai Directions looked straight at Barnaby - straight between the eyes and said, "You know, I really shouldn't be telling you this but the chemical make-up of A Paste and the D Paste are quite different. We go to all sorts of troubles and precautions to try to make sure that the two pastes don't ever mix. If ever the tiniest drop of Class D fell in to the Class A paste, well, that could indeed cause a catastrophe. Yes, a real catastrophe."

"Why, what would happen?" asked Barnaby absolutely spellbound.

"You ever seen an exploding snooker ball," asked Dai. "Not a pretty sight, I can tell you. Not a pretty sight lad"

So, the factory tour continued. They saw the injectors injecting the coloured dye into the squidges of large paste. Next, a huge machine that looked a bit like a wheel with spherical cups attached, scooped up the coloured squidges and moulded them into balls. The metal cups then detached themselves and fell away into a sort of trackway where they rolled into a fiercely burning furnace.

"How long will they stay in there?" asked Barnaby.

"About three hours until they are well and truly cooked." replied Dai. "Look, there are some coming out." At that moment a small but heavy steel doorway opened revealing the scorching heat inside the furnace. A red hot ball appeared , shot a full two metres into the air then dropped into a pool of water. A whoosh of steam rose towards the roof of the building where it was then sucked outside by a large fan.

"Wait there!" exclaimed Dai, "I'll fish one out. You know, I get awfully excited at this point because you never know what colour you'll get until you unscrew the casing." He tried to turn the metal sphere once, then twice, but unsuccessfully. Each time he made the effort his face turned to a shade close to the bottle of red coloured dye on the wall behind him. On the third attempt, he finally succeeded. Three further twists and there it was in his hand - a bright, shiny pink snooker ball.

The visit continued at a fair pace. The group saw the packing centre featuring case after case of large tournament balls and smaller sized cases of children's sized balls. They were shown another moulding system that turned the A Paste into piano keys. The last thing that they saw along their journey was another production line although here, everything appeared to be on a much larger scale.

"Here's our new venture," thundered Dai. "Bowling balls."

The process itself appeared to be exactly the same as that for snooker balls but here everything had been 'supersized'. Also, there were some far more interesting colours paraded in huge bottles along the far wall.

"We are all very proud of this new venture here at The Splendid Snooker Balls Storehouse and we're proud of the fact that our balls will be used at next week's Super Bowl Tournament." Dai had puffed his chest out so far on announcing this that everybody watching was convinced that he was going to explode. "Yes," he continued, "the fruit of this very factory will be seen in use by millions of ten- pin bowling fans right around the world. Now children, our tour is almost over. Just one thing left, the part of the trip that children appear to love the most, the Gift Shop"

In the shop, there were snooker balls both large and small and of course, cues, waistcoats plus all of the paraphernalia attached to the game. There was even a concert grand piano there for sale. Emblazoned on the front, in gold was the company logo, S.S.B.S. Best of all though and the most popular choice for the children were little sets of snooker ball gob-stopper sweets. Later, the children discovered that not only did the reds taste of strawberry and the blacks taste of blackcurrant but they also stained your teeth the same colour. Nobody could figure out the pink ones though but most of the children thought that they tasted curiously of fresh rhubarb.

As they queued to leave the gift shop, Beth managed to catch the attention of Dai Directions. Pulling lightly on his sleeve she asked, "Excuse me Dai. Just one more question. The wall over there, the one where the squidges are squirting from. What is that horrible grinding noise coming from behind the wall?"

"Oh you are a bright one you are, aren't you. Bright indeed. Truth be told though, see, I can't tell you. Well, I could tell you but then I'd have to ki……" and he suddenly stopped himself from giving any more details. Taking a quieter more secretive tone he answered Beth, "I could tell you, but then you'd have to spend the rest of your life here. Trade secret that is. Nobody must ever know what goes into our pastes. Oh no. Not never."

And so it was, that one very bright but mightily mystified little girl joined her joyful gob-stopper chewing friends with their red and green and black tongues. They all appeared to be tickled pink as the luxury coach made its return journey to their quiet little school nestled besides a meandering river. All remained still blissfully unaware of the problems that lay just around a corner in their own particular time lines.

CHAPTER 8.

Elftrafications.

Strange things happened besides the shores of a magical lake in the town of Hope on the night the children returned from their factory visit. Strange things indeed - things that wouldn't be witnessed by any human being. Things that would never have been understood by any normally rational human soul. As the frost formed that night on every single twig and branch, every stubbornly remaining leaf or undiscovered nut gained a crisp coating of ice-capped rime. The water of the lake itself, was initially still and mirror like but swiftly clouded. Dense clinging mist hung over the dark deep water with only the Too-whit Too-whoo of a distant owl passing through disturbing the creepy silence. A starlight sky, together with a dickory-dock moon shining high above slowly disappeared from view behind the wintery vapours of the lake's personally formed misty cloud.

No-one was actually there to witness the magical transformation as the witching hour neared with the exception of the odd bemused badger or a vixen trying to sniff out her route to Jem Simpkins' hen-house. Some squirrels and hedgehogs had indeed been roused from their wintry slumber but after feeling the sense of foreboding lingering heavily in the night air, had wisely felt it best to return to their warm, downy pillows. No person, at least no human person would witness the magical event. This night belonged to the fairy folk and to them alone.

Without warning, small silvery sparks and golden flutters filled the frosty air. Turning and twisting in the misty vapours, creating whorls, spirals, squadrons and skeins. A multitude of magic lights tumbled and danced forming symmetrical reflections on the waveless still water.

Darting, turning, hovering, like starlings in the autumn, moving in millions yet strangely as one, forming wondrous shapes and pattens in the mist. Like a silent symphony, this legion of living light rose for a final time in the mist, then swiftly settled on the northern shore, besides the bare apple and cherry trees, amongst branches of bracken and the first signs of snowdrop shoots announcing the start of Spring.

Not a sound was uttered nor a signal given yet moving as one, the fairy flutters formed a golden circle turning its way majestically through a lakeside glade. On closer inspection of the circle, two lonely sparks appeared to sit near the centre of this bright halo of light.

A skirl of teensy-weensy bagpipes pierced the air - playing a slow, strangely threatening lament. Drums and tabors joined the proud tune, beating out a sad repetitive rhythm. Dum, Dum, dum daddee dum dum. Initially, they kept their place in the background of the orchestra. Soon the beat had entered the hearts, souls, wings, indeed every single feather of each and every member of that gathered throng. Still, the drums beat out their rhythm.

Dum, Dum, dum daddee dum dum.
Dum, Dum, dum daddee dum dum.
Dum, Dum, dum daddee dum dum.

Without warning, the voices of the circle joined the chorus.

Elf
Elf
Elf—tr—fic—a—tion.

Elf
Elf
Elf—tr—fic—a—tion.

Elf
Elf
Elf—tr—fic—a—tion.

Louder and louder the voices increased in rhythmic volume as the mystic circle started to turn, rising, falling and spinning with the relentless rhythm of the chant.

Elf
Elf
Elf—tr—fic—a—tion.

Without any warning, the gathered clan fell to a sudden and complete silence. Once again, only a distant owl could be heard hooting through the frosty air. No signal had been made, nor any order given but all present had fallen silent in unison. The still hush had descended when the band had finally reached the final note of their strangely haunting lament.

Silence embraced the gathered host.

Illuminated only by the golden glow of their fluttering feathers, all eyes were now focused on the two lonely figures sitting in the circle's centre. One looked in complete control of the night's magical event, like a conductor appraising his orchestra or an artist surveying his canvas before adding the final stroke to his emerging masterpiece. The other figure was a complete gibbering nervous wreck – constantly twitching and flinching, scratching and weeping. His eyes were darting through the fairy circle, trying to find one, just one friendly face that would support him through this terrible night. Then slowly at first but swiftly gaining in strength and volume the chant started again until once again the entire glade resounded with the roar.

Elf
Elf
Elf—tr—fic—a—tion.
Elf
Elf
Elf—tr—fic—a—tion.

The Fairy King hovered at the centre of the circle, brimming with confidence, he rose, fluttered his wings and then fell to his feet. Making a swift motion with his arms, he indicated that the ring should be still and at his command so it was. Looking all around the circle, then at the troubled spirit at the centre, he took a deep breath and then addressed his audience, "Class D Fairy - Keith the Teeth, you know why you've been summoned to this gathering of our fairy brotherhood and sisterhood. You know what has been said of you."

"No, I don't know. I've no idea why you've called me here and anyway, whatever it is, I never did it. Never once did I did it, not once," spluttered Keith in reply.

Now, Whatever images you carry in your head about the appearance of fairies, you really must cast them aside when you think of Class D Fairy, Keith the Teeth. He was small, even in comparison with the rest of the fairy folk around him. Small but stocky in stature, as his width almost matched his height. His hair appeared to shoot out of his head in raspberry jam controlled spigots. Even a wintered and withered parsnip looked far prettier than his nose. He appeared to wear the fairy equivalent of a coal miner's donkey jacket, grey, greasy and gloomy. Even his fairy feathers appeared dull, faded and grimy. In comparison to the rest, there was hardly a spark or glimmer to his fairy glow. "What am I supposed to have done anyway," he asked boldly.

Up stepped Master Molar, the other fairy at centre circle, "Done? Done?" he exclaimed. "Don't you even know what you've done?"

"N....no," gibbered Keith. "I've been good I have. A good little fairy like I was always told to be."

"Pointify him!" shouted a lone voice from the crowd, "Aye, Pointify him!" agreed a few others in support.

"No, not yet," stated the Master Molar, firmly quashing the request before it spread, "not until we've heard the full case set before him. Even this wretched creature still deserves his say."

Keith tried to curl himself into the ground wondering whether he could find a mole hole that he could possibly use to escape from his pending trial. Sadly, any underground escape eluded his prying fingers.

"Bring him forth," shouted the Master Molar, "Bring forth The Grinder."

From within the gathered throng a wizened old fellow stepped towards the centre. He was tall, slim and with an air of the eternal mathematician about him. Carrying a clip board and pencil, he looked down over the rim of his bone framed spectacles at poor Keith the Teeth, inspecting him as if he'd discovered something a dog had left behind.

"Do you know this creature?" asked Master Molar.

"Aye," replied The Grinder, "Knows him well I does. Known him since his fledgling flight. He delivers the Class D to the factory, 'least he's s'posed to."

"What do you mean by that?" questioned the Master Molar, "What do you mean by 'least he's s'posed to?"

"Well, Master Molar Sir, tharrun there hasn't brought in a single ivory since the Ones that Walk finished their Festival of Twinkly Lights. Not a single one he hasn't."

A gasp went up from the gathered throng. A collective sucking in of air that almost stole the very last breath of air from that lakeside glade. Again, the chant commenced and grew,

Elf
Elf
Elf—tr—fic—a—tion.
Elf
Elf
Elf—tr—fic—a—tion.

Again, poor Keith searched for a mole tunnel but escape still totally eluded him.

Master Molar quickly silenced the throng with a raised hand and a single violent flap of his wings. Then, holding his head high, called out, "Ivory Cuspid, fetch yourself here child. Stand besides me."

Immediately in direct response to his summons, a fairy flutter occurred at one edge of the ring. One solitary fairy fluttered and rose above the throng and then sped swiftly to answer the summons. She landed between the Master Molar and the Fairy King with all of the grace and elegance that you'd expect from a member of the Class A clan.

"See that child over there," pointed out the Master to Keith. "That child who only gained her permit when the nuts formed and the leaves fell. Since the Ones that Walk finished their Festival of Twinkly Lights, that child there has trebled her collection figure. You know very well, Keith theTeeth how we punish the slacker don't you, how we will not tolerate the bone idle. Indeed, there is no place in the glade for any drowsy dullard. Let me take a moment to describe the punishment to you, the punishment of Elftrification."

Again, the manic chant rose from the glade like the sound of a baying pack of hounds closing in for the kill.

Elf
Elf
Elf—tr—fic—a—tion.

Elf
Elf
Elf—tr—fic—a—tion.

"Silence!" shouted the Master Molar. "All should hear this. Heed this warning Fairy Folk. Heed this well. Heed well the punishment given to the slack fairy, the lazy, the bone-idle. Heed it well."

"Heed it well," came a solitary voice from the mystic multitude.

"SSShhhhhh," came the quelling shushs of the many.

"If found guilty Keith, the punishment of Elftrafication will befall upon your person. You will be dragged from this glade by your ears to complete the first part of the punishment, the Process of Pointification."

"Pointify him!" rang out the solitary voice once again.

"SSShhhhhhhhh," chastened the other members of the circle in response.

"And once it is felt that the correct degree of pointiness of the ears has been achieved we will continue to the process of Costumification. We will bring forth the Red and White Stripy Drawers of Dishonour, the Green Top-coat of Treachery and the Red Floppy Hat of Humiliation. BUT! and I say again BUT! before the process of Costumification is completed, we will undertake the process of Tear-eoff-ication upon your body." Master Molar announced to his by now transfixed fairy audience.

A mighty gasp engulfed the gathered Fairy Folk, creating a current of frosty air so strong that branches of bare winter trees, surged momentarily towards the circle's centre.

"No, please, PLEASE, not Tear-eoff-ication, please. You know, I'm really, really attached to my wings. I know they don't look much but they've all I've got. How will I manage flying without them?" begged Keith. By now, he was besides himself with despair, still prodding the ground trying to find a mole tunnel. "No, please," he squealed, "please don't tear off my wings."

"You will not need wings, not where you're going you lazy scoundrel." Master Molar informed him. Cheers, whoops and yells again hailed from within the gathered crowd. "You will be banished from the clan and chased to the Far North to live out your miserable life in that frozen hell. If you are lucky, and indeed, you'll need to be very lucky, The Man in Red may look down on you with kindness although in my opinion, I don't think he'll touch you with a barge-pole. No more fluttering through the warm summer sunshine. No more lounging besides crackling autumn bonfires. No more homely snuggles under warm pillows smelling of lavender. Oh no. Just snow and frost and wind and the eternal infernal noise of toy making and Ho-Ho-Ho-ing." explained Master Molar to all present.

"Now, before this hideous process proceeds," continued The Master, "I have to ask you if there is anything that you wish to say in your defence? Not that it is likely to change my decision. However, I believe that over the years all former Master Molars throughout the turning seasons have always granted this request. Light entertainment for the masses though if you ask me."

This last piece of information startled Keith and for a moment he stopped prodding the earth. Trying to regain his last ounce of dignity and composure, he fluttered upwards to a standing position and stared the Master Molar square between the eyes.

"Just one thing for you to consider Master." He uttered and pointed a trembling finger directly at the fair Ivory Cuspid and continued, " Her. Right there. That young whippersnapper there. That strumpet that only gained her permit as the last of this year's nuts grew brown. Ask yourselves all of you ," now addressing the gathered throng," Where is SHE getting all HER ivory from? I mean, it stands to reason. Children in her part of the town don't just start losing their teeth twice as often as they once did whilst the children in MY part of the town all decide to keep hold of theirs. Why would they decide to do that? Spite? Meanness? You tell me. "

A tiny unfledged fairy near the front of the ring turned to his mum and said, "He's got a point there mum hasn't he?"

"Sshh," chastised his mum, before placing her hand in front of his mouth. "From the mouths of babes." she thought in self-conscious embarrassment.

"And another thing Mum. Why do we pay more for ivory from some parts of towns and less for others?" continued the young fairy unfazed.

"It's because of what the Ones that Walk eat," whispered his mum. "Some of their diets build better ivory. We can then trade it for more silver. 'tis said though that our spies, The Gentlemen of the Gnome Service have learned that the striplings have come to know of the price difference."

Keith had heard the conversation and realised that if there was a moment to be grasped, then he'd better grasp it now. "Maybe," he suggested, "Just maybe the Ones that Walk have hatched a plan to dupe us out of our silver. Maybe they have broken the Terms and Conditions."

"Not the Terms and Conditions," croaked a wizened white-bearded fairy sitting high in the branches of a bare silver birch. Another gasp rippled out from the throng. This time the sudden inhalation of air within the gathered throng, ruffled feathers around the ring.

"Aye indeed," continued brave Keith the Teeth, "Aye, a Breakification of the Terms and Conditions." Thereupon, once he'd uttered these words, the attitude of the gathered clan changed instantly.

"You tell-em Keith," rang out a single clear voice, and on the spur of the moment, the chant was taken up by the thousands.

You tell-em Keith

You tell-em Keith

You tell-em Keith

Keith The Teeth.

Keith The Teeth.

Master Molar signalled for silence but on this occasion it took a bit more time to calm the confusion down and restore order. The Elders were then quickly summoned to the centre of the circle. Four White-beards, one each from the four quarters of the circle, fluttered forward and formed a huddle. Excited words were exchanged. Viewpoints were put forward, debated and discarded and more new ones introduced. Without warning, Master Molar's voice rang out, "Bring forth the

Terms and Conditions," and a small, spectacled sweetling fluttered forward and handed the gathered Elders an ancient parchment scroll. It was swiftly unrolled and studied in great detail. Fingers pointed, fine points examined at length. Spectacles for the Elders were even summoned. Whispers were heard. "Hhhhmmm." "A-ha." "Maybe the Gnome Service report is true?" Finally, the five faced the ring. Master Molar signalled silence again and stated, "It has been decided that Class D fairy Keith the Teeth may indeed have a point. He may have discovered that a Breakification of the Terms and Conditions has occurred. To that end, we have decided to permit him to maintain his fairy form until the last Hawthorn flower has fallen. Until that time he must spend every waking moment trying to prove that a Breakification has occurred and to identify the individual One that Walks who has caused it. If he should succeed in his quest then this Fairy Circle will reform again to order the Extractification of that individual."

Ex-tract
Ex-tract
Ex-tract-if-ic-a-tion!

chanted the crowd.

Master Molar turned, expecting to see a very much relieved fairy facing him but he was faced with nothing but empty space. Keith the Teeth had finally found his mole hole and at that very moment, he was fluttering for all of his worth along it guided only by his own personal dim but golden glimmer. Keith knew only too well that fairies were fickle folk and that their feelings can swing like a clock's pendulum. As he soared through the subterranean tunnel, just one thought raced through his head, "You can never be sure how these fairy matters will turn out."

CHAPTER 9.

Things that go bump in the day.

The days of winter had continued. Winds and wetness were both routinely present supplemented by thick, thick fog. So far, however, no frosts or deep snows had appeared. At Hope Junior School, nothing ever appeared to change. Even the excitement created by Nigel Rivett's Tooth Fairy wheeze appeared to have blended into a strange, quirky sort of routine normality. Away from the school though, things indeed were changing rapidly. For one tiny tooth fairy, life had become an eternal hunt for hidey holes, mole tunnels and badger sets, constantly looking over his shoulder at wings that hadn't rested in days. Yes indeed, things were changing, but not in Hope though, or in the H.G.G.L. factory or indeed in The Splendid Snooker Balls Storehouse. Even the events at Mr. Simpkins' rat farm and at Dai Dissections' science laboratory still meandered forward in a sad routine of sameness. However, far beyond the town where the river ran clear and sparkling until it eventually reached the glove factory, far from the young lad with now more money than sense and also far away from a frightened fretful fairy, events were about to happen that would certainly stir things up a bit and change people's lives for ever.

Ladies and Gentlemen, you join us here this evening for a recital of piano music by the world renowned performer Vladimir Keybelter accompanied by the London Radio Orchestra and their conductor Sir Rodney Skull. This series of

concerts is being sponsored by S.S.B.S. Ivories who have kindly provided us with a brand new eighty six key, concert grand-piano. The programme commences this evening with a performance of the Grieg piano concerto in A minor, opus 16, but first, we join the audience as they applaud the arrival of the orchestra leader, violinist Fracesci Fiddler.

Polite applause

Silence

And now, appearing from the wings, the conductor for the evening walks to the podium, takes his baton and turns to the audience to acknowledge the rapturous applause.

Rapturous applause.

Silence.

More silence.

Even more silence.

A solitary cough from the upper circle.

A mobile phone's ringtone played a funky little marimba

followed by a massive

Sshhush.

Finally, Vladimir Keybelter takes the stage, strolls confidently towards the ivories, stands between the instrument and the piano stool, flicks the tails on his tail coat upwards as he takes his seat. Uses a similar motion to flick his hair from his eyes, wrings his knuckles to create a huge click then signals to the conductor that he is ready. Sir Rodney raises his baton, Miss Fiddler lightly places her bow to the strings of her splendid antique Vuillaume violin. The conductors baton comes down, a roll of drums fill the concert hall and then, two hands with fingers placed to perfection thrust themselves down onto the pure white keys of the piano.

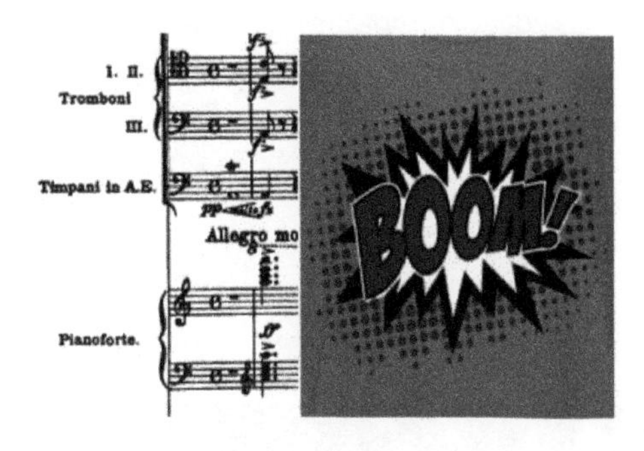

Welcome back after the break viewers to the final frame of Snooker's S.S.B.S. World Championship here at the Tankard Theatre. Going into the final deciding frame the overall match was finely balanced at 7-7 but it now has to be said that Tornado Thomas has taken this final frame by storm. It now looks as though he's going to possibly finish in real style with a maximum 147 break – and take the outright Championship.

Click - roll - perdunk.

(Crisp supportive applause.)

That yellow moves him up to 122

Green next – middle pocket - 125

(Increasingly loud, prolonged applause.)

Down goes the brown! 129 – Just perfect.

(Increasingly louder and very prolonged applause.)

Yes, absolutely perfect. I just don't believe this!

The final frame in a very tight final and he's going for a perfect clear out.

The mark of a true genius.

Blue next - top left pocket – 134

Followed by the Pink – bottom right – 140.

(Rapturous applause, whoops and screams.)

Followed by venue filling pin dropping silence – the last pot.

The frame is already his but he's left himself a tricky shot on the final black, a long shot into the bottom left corner. He'll want to finish on a high but he's going to have to put a lot of spin onto the white as he'll need to screw it back hard to avoid seeing it going in-off. The whole audience are on the edge of their seats in rapt anticipation. Will he finish with a 147?

Welcome everybody to the Twenty Fifth Open Championships live from the eighteen lane bowling centre here at Greater Kegling. This competition is sponsored by S.S.B.S. Bowling Balls, a company, it must be said that is new to the ten pin scene. We're just waiting now for the current ladies champion, Tara Honeybun, to step up to the lane and take her first roll of this special evening. Her she is now. She steps up to her lane, acknowledging a ripple of applause from her fans. She takes a brand new bowling ball, and also takes a large pair of golden scissors to cut a golden ribbon bow to open play at these championships.

I must say, what a curious ball. Pure lily white in colour, almost looking like a giant snooker ball. Easing the ball back, and taking a short run she releases and wow. I don't think I've ever before seen such power put into a ball in the ladies competition. That ball is really running true and straight – looks odds on to be a certain strike.

News of all three explosions travelled far and wide. Vladimir Keybelter never got past the second bar of Grieg's great work. Afterwards, the piano keyboard was virtually unplayable as almost every key was now a black one.

Tornado Thomas' snooker cue was burned to a frazzle as were his eyebrows and lashes. The championship itself had had to be abandoned as any further play on the snooker table was impossible as it had quite a large crater in the green cloth at one end.

Tara Honeybun was in a state of total shock, despite learning that her first ball had indeed scored a strike. The entire back wall of the Greater Keglin bowling centre was now nothing more than a pile of smoking rubble lying in a heap in the back yard.

Yes, news of the three disasters travelled fast, far and wide. It even reached the otherworld; an enchanted glade that lay besides a magical lake at the far side of a town that straddled a fast flowing river.

"I tell thee in truth Master Molar," insisted Grinder. "All them three splosions was caused by a mix up of Class A and Class D ivory."

Master Molar and the summoned fairy Elders shook their heads in disbelief.

"Splosions?" queried Master Molar.

"Aye, splosions. Three of 'em." reported Grinder. " Last one was a right thumper by all accounts. Lucky 'tweren't a deathly if you ask me. 'tis that Cuspid strumpet, you mark me words. Ivory Cuspid's the sweetling wot did it. She was filching teeth from the brown part o' the town and passing it off as Class A ivory."

"So, Master Grinder," queried a Greybeard. "What part did Keith the Teeth have in this sorry story."

"Ah, now there's a tale indeed. A sad, sorry tale. You know, 'tis my belief that he had nothing to do with the mixup at all. Total innocent and look what we nearly done to him. He could be right up there now singing Jingle Bells in the frozen North." whispered Grinder, wistfully nodding his head.

'" Tis the fault o' one o' the Ones that Walk. Checked Cuspid's records didn't I. What sort of fool could think that any stripling child could pillow seventy four teeth in one moonflow? Child would lose so much ivory their head would cave in" stated Grinder emphatically ?

"Tell me Master Grinder?" asked Master Molar. "Do we know of the pillow of this stripling?"

"Aye Master," he replied slowly, nodding his head. "but turns out, there was more than one stripling child involved in this wicked trickery. There has indeed been a 'normous Breakification of the Terms and Conditions."

All the assembled Elders looked gravely at each other, gazing firmly and deeply into each other's eyes, then nodding slowly and as one, uttered just one word in chorus.

"Freezification!"

Thus, in an enchanted glade that lay besides a magical lake the curse was cast.

It was just an ordinary morning for Beth Saunders. Boiled egg and wholemeal toasted soldiers ,followed by orange juice, Earl Grey tea for her breakfast. As always, Beth collected a pocketful of breadcrumbs to feed her two favourite lake ducks. She bade her mum a cheery farewell, grabbed her coat, scarf and gloves then tripped along the garden path, through the gate and onto the path that led to the park. Indeed, for a Monday morning here heart was full of the joys of Spring.

"And don't just carry your coat," shouted Mrs. Saunders, waving from the garden gate. "Wear it. Button it up tight and wrap that scarf around you. Look." she continued, pointing skywards. "Clouds as grey as battleships up there. Could start to snow soon."

The light breeze that Beth had noticed in her garden was starting to become very un-breeze like. In fact, if truth be told they were turning more towards the howling gale level of windiness. It was only as she approached the lakeside that she actually realised that things were not quite right weather-wise. Pausing a while, all at once, her heart filled with a sense of foreboding and doom. Clouds appeared to be taking part in aerial battles, twisting, turning and tumbling in constant cascades and contortions. To accompany this, rain started to fall heavily with the steely cold wind driving it into Beth's face making it feel as though she was being shot at by millions of icy needles. She pulled her hood down hard over her head and for the first time in her young life tied the pull strings into a bow. She noticed another pull string around her waist. With no hesitation now, that was tied hard into another secure bow.

Just as she thought that things couldn't possibly get any worse - they did. The driving rain turned to icy hail with stones about the size of a garden peas. Only one option remained open for Beth now. She turned and ran for the small amount of shelter that the park's band-stand had to offer. Huddling as low as she could get, she hid behind a cast iron pillar finding just enough shelter to survive the winter tempest. Her world had become a deafening roar of freakish, screaming wind and the constant pinging of hailstones hitting the tin roof of the one thing that now appeared to be saving her life, the park band-stand. For a moment, the weather appeared to hold off its ferocious attack giving Beth a moment to peep around her protective pillar. Looking towards the lake, she clearly saw her two ducks take to the air, flapping for all they were worth away towards the South and a safe sanctuary. Something else caught her eye. The clouds – which had already just minutes earlier appeared so troubled, now looked as though they were bringing forth a storm planned in hell itself. Clouds that had been grey now turned black; black as the deepest night. A black so dark that street lights activated but failed to force back the gathering gloom. Then the clouds appeared to sink suddenly towards the lake shore. Next a huge streak of lightning forked across the lake and struck one of the trees on the far shoreline, leaving it shattered, mangled and smoking from the fearful impact. The sight completely tore the breath from Beth's body. The water in the lake appeared to instantly freeze, with the process initially having starting on the Northern shore but spread in seconds right across the lake. So sudden had the frost formed that it even caused its own peculiar sound effect - a mind numbing, deafening shrieking sound, that Beth was sure could not be made by no earthly force.

Snow started falling in huge snowflakes, the size of a small girl's fist. It was driving, drifting snow. Twisting, turning, spinning, filling every inch of space around the lake, the park and deep into the town itself. For many, many years after, the folk of Hope Town would remember this snowfall. They would recollect where they had been when it fell, remember who had been with them and also sadly recount the friends and family members that had been taken by the Great Blizzard as it became known. As for Beth, on many occasions besides Christmas trees and firesides, she would share the story with her own children and then her grandchildren. She'd tell them how her mother had desperately searched for her through the driving blizzard. How her mum had finally found her, huddled near a corner of the bandstand and of how her mum had scooped her up in her motherly arms. Protecting Beth on the journey home by cuddling her close to her body, her mum had struggled through the snow-drifts to the safety and warmth of their cosy home besides the park.

The little snow covered school besides the river stayed closed for six whole weeks. Snow had fallen so deep that it was literally impossible to get inside the building. The blizzard had driven the snow into curiously shaped drifts around the houses. Sometimes, when it continued to snow, large areas of the school yard remained snow free whilst a huge drift would form around doors and windows blocking entry and stopping any daylight from entering the classrooms. Inside, despite the best efforts of Mr. Pendry the caretaker, it was impossible to heat and keep the school warm. Water pipes and toilets froze solid. Icicles actually formed on the ceiling of Mr Fortitude Jones' classroom. Had the school stayed open, then no doubt the children would have discussed one other curious phenomenon that had taken place. It appeared that tooth fairy money had literally and for no apparent reason had stopped being delivered. Teeth were optimistically placed under pillows at bed time and to the dismay of many children the very next morning, they would be lying there still.

Many of the families in the lower part of Hope suffered genuine hardship that winter. The H.G.G.L. factory had to close down and lay off their workers as carrying out the work became virtually impossible. Even the dreaded spruddging tank froze solid. At that time of year the river beyond the glove factory would have been running sparkling clear had it not been for the fact that it had entirely become a solid white glacier like mass of frozen water. On occasions, when the weather improved a little, people would remember the eerie silence that would settle like a shroud on the town. No traffic moved. No factory noises. None of the cheery banter created by the children as they walked their different ways to school. Nothing - just eerie silence punctuated by the occasional sound of icicles tinkling to the floor.

No work meant no pay and as a result, hunger held a cold boney finger over the poor people of the lower town. Even old Ma Spruddge found her pure collection business at a complete standstill. After all, have you ever thought how hard it is to find dog mess when the snow is deep enough to cover the tops of your boots? One day, however, when the Spruddges were almost down to their final grains of porridge, there was a knock on the door. Barnaby and Ma had stared at each other in total shock. Neither of them could remember the last time that anybody had knocked on the door of the Spruddge household. Instantly, Ma Spruddge had reached for the rolling pin and dashed to the door.

"WHOSETHATOUTSIDEHADBETTERGOAWAYORILLBRAINY OU." screamed Ma.

"It's only me," came a lonely voice from beyond the door, "Me. Jem. Can I come in? It's freezing out here."

Ma pulled the door open and there indeed was a well lagged Jem Simpkins freezing at the opening. Without warning, a threatening, thundery rumbling sound came from above. Quick as a flash Ma grabbed the toothless Jem Simpkins by the shoulder and pulled him inside just avoiding a mighty avalanche of snow sliding off the roof. They both gazed in wonderment at the half blocked doorway then turned to catch a glimpse of each other's toothless smiles.

"I was just wondering whether you two would like to join me for lunch." queried a frozen Mr. Simpkins. "One of my girls got frosted over and didn't make it through the night but she'll serve up nicely with some sage and onion and gravy."

So it was that through those wicked weeks of bitter winter, Barnaby, Ma and Jem would pass their time staring into the firelight's flickering flames, spinning yarns, reminiscing and telling stories of days and people past. An old rickety rocking chair had been carried from a bedroom and placed near the fire. Occasionally Barnaby took his turn at rocking slowly, feeling his sleepy head droop, enjoying the cozy company and the cuddled up feeling - putting thoughts of the cold frozen world outside clear out of his head. There was no doubt in Barnaby's mind, that his life, and his mother's that winter, had been saved by Old Jem Simpkins and his warm, comfortable cottage hidden behind his rat farm.

As the Arctic ice-age continued and the school remained totally frozen, Barnaby would often be sent out on life-saving missions to gather logs and brushwood from the forest beyond the lake. Jem had taken some old cages and had fashioned for him a simple sledge of sorts. It was frail and flimsy and would never have survived serious downhill sledging but it was just about OK for carrying a few logs back to the cottage fireside. Barnaby been warned and warned not to step onto the frozen lake but he had discovered a new winter sport. If you took a flat stone and skimmed it over the ice, a peculiar shrieking sound would fill the frosty air, echoing through the bare trees of the nearby forest. Occasionally, when he'd run out of stones, he'd gaze up at Beth's house wondering how she was coping with the conditions. Was she staying at home or had she, like many of the other posh folk, flown away to the sun? Sometimes on his *gathering winter fuel* visits he was sure he'd seen lights shining and movement at the posh house on the hill but he couldn't be certain.

Weeks passed slowly until one day it appeared that the worse of the winter was indeed over. Barnaby's normal route to the park walked over bare ground more often than melting slush. His rickety sledge was now almost useless and remained hanging from the cottage wall. Sunlight bore down on the melting lake water as the welcome thaw continued. Barnaby had collected just a few logs and had set them in a pile ready for the long walk back when he looked up and noticed a different shade of white traced out in a nearby lakeside glade. Here, a patch of grass showed through the melted snow and a cheery drift of snowdrops held their heads up to the sky.

"Fair Maids of February," thought Barnaby. "That's what my dad used to call them." Then he took another look at the drift of snowdrops. At first, Barnaby couldn't quite believe what he was actually seeing. He blinked several times in disbelief. The still frosty air had caused tears to form in his eyes. Wiping away those tears, he gazed again at what he simply knew couldn't be true.

Instantly, he dropped a log he'd been holding and set off as fast as his legs would carry him, around the lake, past the bandstand, between the swings and the slide and on to the path that led to Beth's house. He knocked the door furiously and called out "Beth, Beth. Are you in?"

"What on earth is all this commotion?" questioned Mrs. Saunders as she opened the door. "Oh, it's you, what on Earth is the matter young Spruddge?"

Barnaby caught a glimpse of Beth at the end of a carpeted corridor. Moving his head to the side of Mrs Saunders, he spoke to Beth urgently. "Beth. Down besides the lake. You have just got to come and see this. You won't believe it." Then remembering his place and feeling a pair of hostile eyes above him, he gazed up at Beth's mum. "Mrs. Saunders, really sorry about bursting in like this, but can you come too? You really must see this."

The trio trudged through the melting snow and mud, finally making their way back to the lakeside glade. They were urged on by an insistent Barnaby saying things like, "Just over there." and "Not far now." Finally they arrived at their destination..

"Snowdrops." cried Beth. "You dragged us all this way through the mud and slush to see snowdrops.You barmy or what?"

"No, look again," babbled Barnaby. "Step over here. It's easier to see if you get the angle right."

"Oh gosh," exclaimed Mrs. Saunders. "Look Beth, he's right. Just look."

All three gazed in wonder, not at the snowdrops, but at what they appeared to be saying. They were arranged so that they actually spelt out the words of a message.

"It says, *Always read the terms and conditions.*" read Beth out loud as her eyes followed a long snowdroppy formed arrow pointing its way towards a small but perfectly formed grey pebble. She carefully picked up the pebble from the earth. Underneath lay a tiny parchment scroll, faded brown, yet looking strangely new. Carefully, she unrolled it as Mrs. Saunders and Barnaby squeezed in beside her to take a look at this apparent treasure. Barnaby could just about make sense of the tiny letters but beautifully formed copper-plate handwriting. He instantly recognised the two Fairy rule verses that his mother had taught him but as Beth unrolled a little more, he saw a third verse. Squinting hard to make sense of the text, he raised his voice and read it out loud.

Fairy silver, if truth be told
it's for the child alone to hold.
A child will fall in serious trouble
forgetting that teeth are non-refundable.

"It's Tooth Fairy verse," whispered Barnaby.

"Not very good poets are they." stated Beth in a far from impressed and indignant voice.

Mrs. Saunders squinted at the scroll. "Bring that back to the house Barnaby. We'll take another look at that over a cup of tea.

A few minutes later and they were back in Beth's garden. Sounds of tea making wandered towards them from the kitchen. The garden lay dank and bare after the Winter's weather. The only garden colour was the sight of a single weather-beaten garden gnome, fishing beside a small pond.

"Oh, what's this?" whispered Barnaby. As he unrolled the scroll, another tiny piece of paper fluttered to the ground. Quickly gathering it before the breeze took it away.

"Handwriting is different on this one,"noted Barnaby. "Neater if you ask me." Squinting at the tiny writing, he read out.

Beware you ones that walk.
We can freeze your very liver, causing you to shake and shiver.
We'll numb and chill your world with just one spell.
We can cause such monstrous harm to every home or farm,
to every place, no matter where you dwell.
We only need a tooth, that ones you loose in youth.
be it clean or filled or rotten, we don't care.

Just stick besides our rules, because we simply are not fools.
Don't lie, don't cheat and never mess with us."

Winter now is over and past
but it could return. Awf'lly fast.
Don't mess with our silver
stand by our rules.
We may be tiny
but we are not fools.

"Here we are. A nice cup of tea? You two OK? Barnaby? Beth?" asked Mrs Saunders. "You both look like you've seen a ghost."

"No, we're OK, " replied Barnaby, eyes still bulging and jaw almost on the floor. Beth stood by his side, squinting at the fairy message with exactly the same expression. "any chance of a custard cream mum?" she eventually managed to say. Then, almost as if none of this had happened, they slowly made their way past the pond to stand at the edge of the garden, overlooking the lake.

"Pssst.....Sprudgey. Do you think it was the fairies that did it then?"

"Did what?" whispered Barnaby in reply.

"Brought us that Winter. Nearly killed me did that Winter. Almost froze to death."

"Possibly. After all, people said that it was the worse Winter anybody had ever known."

"The news people always said that it was worse in our town than anywhere else." added Beth. "You know, if the fairies did cause that Winter, it's a shame that we can't pay them their money back."

Barnaby whispered low, "We could pay some of it back. I've still got some of it. Well, about half of it I suppose."

"How did you manage that?" asked Beth.

"Rivet asked me to look after it for him. He didn't want his mum to find it because she was always tidying his room, so he asked if he could leave it with me. He said that my mum would never find it because she never cleans up. He said that it was a bit like offshore banking, but I don't know what he meant by that. It's in a shoebox in my bedroom."

"Can you sneak out tonight?" asked Beth, whispering low. "Meet me beside the lake, by the snowdrops...... at midnight. Bring the money....and a spade. Hopefully we can start to put things straight."

If only they had looked back towards the house. Maybe they would have spotted a tiny change in the fisherman gnome. His look of concentration on his rod and reel had gone. Instead, his face was fixed in the sort of expression people have when they are starting to listen to and make sense of every word overheard. His fishing rod now lay across his lap. In his hands now you could see, had you looked, a tiny notepad. In less than a blinkling of an eye, he took a well chewed pencil from behind his ear and wrote a short message. He gave a shrill short whistle. Suddenly a tiny robin flew down and took a teeny-weeny scrap of paper from his gnarled and grimy hand. Finally, in the second half of the blinkling of that same eye, the gnome regained his original pose, once again, endlessly hoping for a catch with his fishing rod.

And so it was, that the couple met at midnight, in moonlight, making a small hole and placing inside it a battered shoebox, heavy with the weight of fairy silver. They covered it with a little earth and placed a pile of pebbles on top of their treasure.

CHAPTER 10.

Fifteen Moonflows Later.

"Well now, Barnaby Spruddge." greeted Beth. "Didn't expect to see you here at my favourite lake. What are you doing here? Fishing?"

Barnaby had actually jumped a mile with Beth's sudden appearance. She had managed to really startle him. He'd been so lost in one of his daydreams he'd been totally unaware of her sudden arrival. She'd actually sneaked up from behind a hedge and then surprised him. Looking up at her whilst regaining his composure, he couldn't stop himself blushing. "Just thinking some thoughts." he answered in an effort to mask his complete surprise and shock.

"Carry on thinking them thoughts, but if it's OK with you, I'll share this bench with you a while." Beth neatly folded her skirts gently around her knees and sat down in a most ladylike manner. Fumbling inside her pockets she took out some bread-crumbs and on doing so knew exactly what would be happening next. "Hope you don't mind me saying this Spruddgey, but you are looking much smarter these days. What's happened to you?"

Barnaby in humbly accepting her compliment nodded his head and answered, "Aye indeed. Things have improved. Ma's got a new boyfriend and he's really looking after us well. You must know him. Old Jem Simpkins, the rat man. She's a different person now."

"Is it true, what they say about him," asked Beth, "That he has a really sweet little cottage around the back of that old tin shed?"

"Correct." nodded Barnaby, "It would be just perfect if it wasn't for his garden gnomes. They really give me the squeegees they do. I often think when I pass them that they're wa..." He faltered and thought better of completing the sentence.

Beth gasped anyway, "All those rats and you worry about a few garden gnomes? What's wrong with you?"

Two ducks sailed in towards them on the lake. Beth tore some crumbs from a slice of bread and threw them at their hungry beaks. "Meet two of my best friends," stated Beth. "The brown one is called Lizzy and the coloured one is called Frankie. Remember what Mr. Jones taught us about the Spanish Armada?"

"Ahh." nodded Barnaby. "Queen Elizabeth and Francis Drake. Clever."

Without speaking they watched them dabbling and quacking merrily for quite a while and then continued their conversation.

"You know, he's really fallen on his feet after the rock music scare." continued Barnaby.

"What rock music scare?" asked Beth.

"It was the scientific guys. Somebody suggested that teenagers who listen to too much loud rock music get cancer in the brain." Barnaby scratched his nose, then continued. "Personally, I think it's a load of nonsense, but old Jem is doing really well out of it."

"Sorry, you've lost me." Stated Beth totally puzzled.

"Well," continued Barnaby. "It means that they have to do lots of testing and for that, they need loads of rats. He's making a real fortune out of them. Funny thing is, I'm pretty sure that there's nothing in it, so his rats are living the high life, bopping along to The Rolling Stones and The Who. All well fed, watered and in the groove. Can you imagine the picture – rats on Top of the Pops?"

"You are kidding me?" queried Beth.

"Look at what I'm wearing Beth. He's making really sure that Ma, me and himself are all doing well out of the lab rats. Only last week he took himself an Ma down to the dentist to get themselves fixed up with false teeth. I can hardly recognise my mother. I can hardly recognise myself. Never, ever thought I'd get sick of having eggs for breakfast."

Beth said nothing but simply gave his a quizzical look.

"Now there's going to be a wedding isn't there," mumbled Barnaby.

"A wedding?" gasped Beth.

"Aye. A wedding. He asked Ma to marry him. Only wants me to be the Best Man don't they. I've got to help organise it to. What do I know about weddings? Clueless I am. I don't do speeches."

Suddenly, a hectic flurry of nearby feathers splashed a shower of water towards them as Lizzy and Frankie fought over a particularly tasty crumb. Beth and Barnaby had to wipe some lake water spray from their eyes. "See those blue flowers over there?" queried Barnaby pointing to a glade just off the opposite shore.

"Bluebells I think." responded Beth without being totally certain.

"Aye, but not any old bluebells Beth. Can't you see? Come on, we'd better go and check it out."

So the curious looking procession started. Barnaby in the lead with Beth following closely alongside him. She occasionally threw the two ducks a piece of stale crust to ensure they kept up with them. Despite being breathless, half way around the lake, Beth burst into song.

"In and out the dusty bluebells,
In and out the dusty bluebells,
In and out the dusty bluebells,
Who shall be my partner?"

They were both completely out of breath when they finally raced into the glade and began to look around. "There's nothing here," shouted Beth, shaking her head in disbelief. "Just ordinary bluebells. What did you think you saw to make them special anyway?"

"No, there is something, not as clear as the snowdrops last year I'll grant you, but there is something. Come up here." As he spoke, Barnaby continued to climb onto the low hanging bough of an old gnarled oak tree. He then held out his hand and pulled Beth to his side. "Now," he stated in explanation for his actions. "Look down on them."

Beth nearly fell off the bough of the tree in shock. Another flowery fairy message was clearly visible in the bluebells from the height they were at. Even more curious than the first one had been.

"Change in the terms and conditions." read Beth, then shouted, "What on earth does that mean? Oh, look there's the pebble. Help me down."

Beth clambered down, then helped her friend to ground level. She noticed him looking upwards again. "What are you looking at now?" she questioned.

"Up there," replied Barnaby. "Top of the oak tree. Mistletoe. I'll have to remember that come Christmas time. Money in the bank that is."

"Mistletoe?"

"Aye Mistletoe. Folks will pay good money for a sprig of mistletoe come Christmas. They do say that folks ...."

"I know what they say that folks do under mistletoe," nodded Beth and at the same time she pulled Barnaby until they were both directly under the largest of the clumps of mistletoe.

"Tappity tappity on your shoulder," she sang."You shall be my partner," and she reached towards him and kissed him, just a little peck, fondly on the cheek.

Barnaby thought he'd been hit by a train and he blushed the biggest blush in all of his young life – a dream coming true.

"Now then," smiled Beth broadly. "Where's that pebble?"

Underneath it, they quickly discovered the tiny scroll. To the both of them in outward appearance it looked as ancient as time itself but was strangely new. Huddling together, they squinted at the tiny well-formed handwriting. Without prior knowledge of unfolding events, they wouldn't have known that a fourth verse had very recently been added to the fairy rhyme. It read,

When the fairy leaves some dough
it's for the child alone to stow
No matter from where the tooth do come
For all, half-a-pound will be the sum.

"They really are rubbish poets aren't they." concluded Beth in some dismay.

They took the tiny scroll and wandered back to the waiting ducks at the water's edge. "Hey, I'd better get home now. Mum will worry about me. She worries about me a lot since the blizzard." Said Beth finding a reason to return home. Barnaby gave an understanding nod in response. "Tell me though," she asked. "Would you like a hand with the wedding? I could help out and my mum loves to organise things like that. She always loves a bit of a bash?"

"Your mum help out with the wedding? She'd never want to do that. I mean, after all Beth. You two really are a bit posh aren't you." Said Barnaby, half teasing gently, half matter of fact in recognition of their different backgrounds.

"And you, Spruddgey are going to become the step-son of a very respectable businessman from this little town of ours. Trust me, and trust my mum. Everything will be just hunky-diddly-doo. And always remember. Never underestimate the power of a posh girl. Never." Beth concluded with apparent and growing determination.

"Will you please stop pacing up and down the aisle." suggested old Jem Simpkins – whilst at the same becoming increasingly concerned himself. "After all, it's supposed to be me that's nervous, not you." Simpkins concluded.

"She's late," whispered Barnaby. "She can't be late. Things will start going wrong and I'll get the blame."

Jem took Barnaby firmly by the arm and disagreed. "Brides are always late. It's the thing that brides do. Anyway, still five minutes to go." He glanced nervously at his watch for the eighth consecutive time in the last ten minutes. "Still five minutes to go," he confirmed.

Barnaby was amazed at just how many people had turned up. It was as if everybody that had touched their lives somehow was present in the chapel. There was Mr. and Mrs. Lewis from the bakery. Mr. Fisher from the newsagents. He glanced towards the back and was shocked to see what could only be Mr. and Mrs. Fortitude Jones. Staring directly at Beth, who was sat in the third row, he mouthed the words, "Who invited all these people?" but Beth in response just shrugged and grinned knowingly.

Without warning, the chapel door burst open. Everybody in the congregation turned and stared.

"Dai. Dai Dissections." beamed Barnaby in growing astonishment.

"Hush now boy. It's not Dai Dissections today. Or Dai Directions." corrected a mightily ruffled Dai. "Today I'm wearing my best wedding day suite and tie. Dai Devotions today, that's me. Wedding photography and musician extraordinaire."

"How did this happen?" queried a puzzled Barnaby.

"Quite easy really," confirmed Dai. "Jem here got in touch to see if I could do this for him. Then once I'd agreed, a charming young lady called Miss Saunders confirmed all the details."

Barnaby looked into the chapel. There was Beth and Mrs. Saunders, both looking fantastic sat in their Sunday best. Beth caught his eye, winked and gave him a cheery wave.

"I'll sit over by there Jem," chirruped Dai and proceeded to walk carrying his old, weather-beaten suitcase to the organ stool. When Dai opened up the suitcase, Barnaby saw piles of old camera bits inside, lying next to some kind of ancient squeeze-box type of instrument.

"Ahem," coughed Hoskins the minister. "Apparently the bride has arrived."

Turning to Dai, he gave a supportive nod and then took his place in front of the altar. All at once, the chapel was filled with the strange but strident tones of a moth-eaten, wheezy squeezebox. Beth had by then walked to Dai's side, placed her hand on his shoulder and waited for his signal before raising her voice to the song.

Come write me down
ye powers above.
The man that first created love.

For I've a diamond in my eye
where all my joys and comfort lie.
Where all my joys and comfort lie.

The chapel door gently opened and in walked Sophie Spruddge. Barnaby simply couldn't believe it. Was this really his old Ma, the woman with the rolling pin often seen carrying a scoop and bucket? Her hair was arranged to perfection, standing high on her head in a sort of raised bun, making her look even taller than she actually was. Wisps of curled hair hung down highlighting her face, showing off a charming sweet smile rather than her normal gummy empty mouth. Wearing a long pale blue gown and carrying a bouquet of sparkling white roses she walked down the centre of the tiny church aware of the fact that every single pair of eyes was on her.

The sight of Ma all dressed up quite took Barnaby's breath away. He was seeing his old Ma in a completely new light. For the very first time in his life, he stood tall and felt remarkably proud of her.

Bethany chapel was never big enough to carry a tower of bells but Hope Town rang with music on the day that Mr. and Mrs. Simpkins stepped into the bright sunlight for the first time as man and wife. Dai Devotion continued playing a jaunty jig on his wheezy squeezebox. Voices from old Stanley Spruddge's spruddging crew also helped to fill the air in celebration. They had all brushed up nicely in their very best Sunday dress and had formed a Guard of Honour holding their spruddges over the bride and groom as they made their way to their wedding breakfast. Barnaby didn't know whether anybody else had noticed but he certainly had. Thankfully every single spruddge had been especially well cleaned for this very special task. Smiling and waving at their friends, trying not to get too much confetti in their face, the happy couple came to the second part of the Guard of Honour. All of Jem's garden gnomes had been painted and spruced up and now stood in a proud parade, outlining the path to the chapel vestry. A cold shiver ran through Barnaby's spine when he saw the ranks of gnomey fishermen and gardeners defining the path ahead. As he made his way past them he was still sure that each one was staring directly at him. Suddenly and thankfully for Barnaby, distracting voices rang out.

See the merry Spruddgers swirl,
we made some gloves for a gorgeous girl
to wear upon her wedding day
paid for with cash from our last pay-day.

"Somebody else hopeless at poetry," thought Beth to herself on hearing the words.

Drawing attention to himself with a polite cough, C.S.O. Cedric Sponger stepped out of the Guard of Honour and addressed the bride. "Something for you on this special day Sophie." and he handed her a beautiful pair of white leather gloves. "H.G.G.L.s finest they are my dear. Trust me, you'll look grand wearing those."

"Photographs now please. All of you now. Photographs please." cried wedding photographer extraordinaire Dai. "If you could all just line up over by there now in a minute please. I won't take long now – everybody smiling please."

Dai's photoshoot did, however, appear to take forever, particularly as he appeared to be using some really ancient camera kit. He kept on mumbling things about F stops and aperture settings. People started to look bored and fidgety but then thankfully the extended wait was all over.

"If you'd all like to follow us now," shouted Beth in order to gain the attention of all present. As she spoke the whole party, breathed a collective sigh of hunger relief at the thought of a sit down and some free food and drink approached. Barnaby sidled over to Dai and for a while just watched him loading his antique cameras into his equally antique suitcase.

"Passed down to me by my dad," mentioned Dai proudly. "See that one boy?" and he held up what appeared to be a tiny bashed about black box. "Took that to the war in North Africa he did. Been half way around the world has that camera."

"So, are you still working down at the snooker ball factory Dai?" queried Barnaby.

"Aye, still do a bit there I do. Changed a bit now though. Product range has changed a lot since the three explosions. Heard about the bangs didn't you?"

"Didn't everyone?" replied Barnaby.

"Nasty they were those explosions. Now, they don't make the snooker balls for big competitions any more. Also finished with piano keys and bowling alley balls," said Dai as if some sort of final judgement. He continued to make a familiar air sucking noise through his teeth as he spoke, "Oh certainly not bowling balls." he stated, nodding his head in some finality. "Cutlery" he smiled, "Cutlery, now, there is the future for you. Come, I'll show you. I've bought a set for your mum and your new dad." and he guided Barnaby between the sinister gnome parade and into the vestry.

"There, look you now," said Dai as he pointed to a smart leather bound case placed in the middle of a pile of wedding gifts. "Look at these now. Tidy these are," and he opened the lid. "See. Bone handles." Barnaby gazed at a charming set of knives, forks and spoons, all with gleaming white handles. "Gleaming snooker ball white handles too." added Dai.

"Marvellous," smiled Barnaby. "Tell me, do they make any other colours?"

"Colours?" queried Dai. "Oh colours. Well not now, but I think they could in the future.....red, yellow, green, even pink and black I suppose." and he gave Barnaby a knowing wink.

"Hey Spruddgey!" came a voice from clear across the room. Smiling at him, Beth continued, "it's time for your speech."

"Oh no," mumbled Barnaby. "I've been dreading this."

"Come on now lad,' whispered Dai, "you can do this. If you like, I'll sit just by you and sort of prompt you along. Would that help?"

Barnaby smiled and nodded, "Yes indeed. That would really help. Thanks Dai." and they both wheedled their way through the guests and took their place at the top table.

"Thank everybody for coming," whispered Dai.

So Barnaby did just that. "Easy," he thought. "First bit done."

"Now, say how lovely your mum looks." whispered Dai.

"That's easy," thought Barnaby. "I'll just tell the truth because today she really does look gorgeous."

"Tell them how well she has looked after you since your dad….."

"What, even the rolling pin?" whispered Barnaby.

"It's a Best Man's speech. You're supposed to make people laugh," whispered Dai.

So Barnaby did just that and in no time at all he had everybody rolling with laughter. All in all, he thought he was doing a pretty good job.

"Don't forget to thank the bridesmaid," whispered Dai.

Shaking his head, Barnaby whispered in response, "There isn't one."

"The young lass over there. The one that can't take her eyes off of you. Her and her mum helped to organise all of this, Good as a bridesmaid if you ask me." whispered Dai.

So Barnaby did just that and for once, he managed to look Beth Saunders square in the eyes as he spoke without actually blushing.

"One last thing," added Barnaby. "A huge Spruddge / Simpkins thank you to Mr. Lewis and his bakers for providing us with a wedding cake that can only be described as pure genius." and all eyes turned towards the back of the hall. There, on a silver platter was the biggest chocolate eclair that the town of Hope or indeed possibly the world had ever seen. On the top, appeared tiny caricatures of two rats. One in a fabulous blue wedding gown and the other in morning suite and top hat.

"Just one more thing Mrs. Simpkins," shouted Beth as events came to a happy closure. "You have to turn around and throw your bouquet over your head, and I'm going to catch it." She announced with genuine conviction and anticipation.

"Oh no you're not," stated her mum. "This one's mine."

CHAPTER 11.

And most of them lived happily ever after.

Around the time of the surprising yet well celebrated Simpkins wedding, things started to change in the little town of Hope. It turned out that Dai's prophetic words concerning the future had indeed been right. The new cutlery sets proved to be very popular indeed and had started selling in huge numbers throughout the land and father afield. What had been the old snooker ball factory had to expand in response to growing demand. As a direct result many former spruddgers, manglers and spongers found new, cleaner, safer and better paid jobs – without moving from Hope. The H.G.G.L. factory continued to make gloves (including white ones) but scientists had discovered newer and more efficient methods to tan the leather. This process also involved using far kinder synthetic materials. Nobody needed to collect the revolting *Pure* any more – though this did leave Ma without a sideline job. The whole town was pleased to see the river return to its former glory, running fresh and clear before and beyond the previously hated pollution from the glove factory. With passing time, fishermen could be seen casting flies, trying to catch leaping trout along an increasingly green and charmingly pleasant river bank. Thankfully, this welcome change didn't affect the newlywed Sophie Simpkins in the longer term. She adapted to change and her new role and found a position helping with the accounts, for many years working alongside her devoted husband and his 'beloved' rats.

One day, a few months after the wedding, Barnaby, Sophie and Jem were searching through the old Spruddge household, clearing out and searching for any items that might actually be of use to them in their new lives in the Simpkins cottage. They had almost cleared out the last of their meagre belongings, when Barnaby came across an old, dusty, leather bound case. Pulling it from the depths of a bedroom cupboard and on prising it open he called out, "Ma. Ma. Look what I've found."

Ma, turned quickly to look across the room. "Well, I'll be jiggered," she exclaimed, eyes popping to the size of pomegranates. "That's a real treasure. Lor above. Where did you find that? I thought my old mother had sold that off years ago when she was short on rent money." She took the discarded 'treasure' carefully from Barnaby, wiped off the dust with her sleeve, then gently opened the leather case. Inside, lying within green felt lining lay a dark, ebony clarinet, completely festooned with bright silver keys. "Will you look at that. I wonder. Now I've got these new teeth, will I be able to play still?"

And she could play. Boy, could she play. After a little practice, she joined Discordant Dai's Dixy Dance Band, a jazzy little quartet that specialised in weddings, ceilidhs, birthday, bar mitzvah and Christmas parties.

Eventually in the great order of things the young children of Hope got to terms with the fact that they were all being treated equally by the fairies. Fifty pence for each tooth became the universally accepted norm, just like the fairy verse had said. Just between us, a number of the posh children up in the high part of town were a bit put out when they realised that they were no longer getting a better deal. However, as one generation finished losing their first teeth and the next generation started losing theirs, the dismay over the cash difference became a thing of the past. It was a mere brief blip on the children's timeline in the town of Hope; one that was swiftly forgotten and seldom mentioned – as it had itself became folklore.

Keith the Teeth did really well after everything had settled down and the price of ivory had been set in pebble once again. For the rest of fairy time he became a mystic character that other fairy folk, especially the little sweetlings always looked up to, despite the fact that in stature he was tiddly tiny compared to most other fairies.

You'll remember, I told you right at the start of this chapter that it ended happily for most of our characters. What actually happened to Ivory Cuspid quite frankly, is too horrible to describe and I really wouldn't want to spoil such a happy ending, BUT every year, at Christmas time, if you come across an elf with particularly pointy ears, give her a smile and a kind word. She's been through an awful lot after all.

With renewed effort and focus Barnaby did well and prospered during his school days. He also thrived living in a cheery cottage behind the rat farm with the only blot on his personal horizon being the routine searching stares of Jem's garden gnomes. Despite his increased maturity and self-confidence those squeegee feelings would somehow never leave him.

One day, when he was about fourteen, he'd been sent for a haircut. He'd started using the salon that Ma had used for her wedding, the *Kurl Up and Dye* salon. It was a ladies' salon near to Fisher's newsagents. They didn't mind Barnaby or any other gentlemen popping in for a trim though – any business was still business. One day, Sarah, the owner had asked him, "Do you fancy a Saturday job Barnaby? I need somebody to sweep up and make teas and coffees for my clients. Do you think you can manage that?" So it was, that Barnaby started in the world of real work. Real work that paid real money and this time he really didn't care about the colour of the coins that ended up in his pocket.

He was just coming to the end of his shift one day when he saw someone outside approaching the salon. He recognised a face that he hadn't actually seen or indeed missed seeing in years. Over time he'd often thought of what had become of Nigel Rivett. He had recollected that he had never returned to school after The Blizzard. Nobody really knew what had become of him. Whispers and rumours had said that he'd moved to a new home down the road in Faith but nobody was really sure. There he was though, plain as daylight, walking up the high street towards the salon. Rivett looked towards the salon and spotted Barnaby, holding his brush. Rivett had initially started to smile but stopped himself when he'd recognised his old comic swopping buddy. He then turned away from the salon window and hurriedly crossed the road, clearly wanting to avoid the chance encounter from developing any further . Rivett's smile had actually made Barnaby's blood run cold though. It reminded him of his old Ma, back in her porridge stirring days. It now actually looked as though there wasn't a single tooth anywhere in Rivett's mouth.

The brief strange encounter had brought back many memories to Barnaby's mind though. Chilling memories of Rivett's underhand comic wheeler dealings. Vivid memories of teeth and ivory changing hands over a makeshift playground desk. Clearer still, memories of money being made from what apparently was nothing at all.

A strange thought began to grow in his head as he gathered his sweepings into a pile near the bin. Looking up, he turned to Sarah the stylist and asked her quizzically, "Sarah. Where does all this hair go?"

"Where does it go?" she asked. "Goes in the bin of course. No good to anything is that. Why are you interested? Does your mattress need stuffing?"

And so it is to this very day, if you ever make your way to Hope Town, you will now find not one but two factories standing alongside the banks of a jewel blue river. You will see the original Hope Gloves for Gentrified Ladies factory, still turning out high quality fashion gloves and accessories for the rich and famous everywhere. However, next to it, you'll see a newer and more recently constructed factory and there you'll also notice a freshly painted sign above its main gate:

Barnaby and Beth Spruddge
Quality Art Supplies.
Paintbrushes for daubers, dabblers and artisans everywhere.

ABOUT THE AUTHOR.

Philip Edwards retired from teaching back in 2013. Since then he has become a keen gardener, plays for three Morris dance sides and has become a grandfather to four and an almost.

As a child, he lived in the village of Ferndale in the Rhondda Valley in South Wales. Together with his brother and cousins, then became the first generation from a long family line to escape the clutches of working underground.

The idea for this story came from a throw-away remark on a radio comedy. Somebody said, "If only we could speculate on the tooth fairy market." That sowed the seed of an idea in my head. Twice a day whilst walking his little terrier, Alfie, the story built and built to include its many quirky twists and turns.

Incidentally, if you know Ferndale or fancy taking a trip there, you will still be able to trace Beth's and Barnaby's walk to school. Oh, and back in the 1960s, Ferndale did have a rat farm and a morgue, and my brother regularly made bus trips with cages of rats, taking them to meet their doom.

Philip Edwards

Lightning Source UK Ltd.
Milton Keynes UK
UKHW011440090620
364709UK00003B/610